About Halfway Through
the Game, It Happened . . .

I dropped back. All my receivers were running down field. Charlie was covering Curt, but Curt had a step or two on him. All my other receivers were covered. I drew back and passed to Curt.

Charlie raced after Curt. Curt jumped for the ball. Everybody watched.

At that very instant—timed down to the second—Neal and Doug both rushed me.

Suddenly Neal had me by the shoulders. Only, instead of trying to throw me to the ground like he usually did, he was holding me up. Real straight.

And just as he had me standing up—stretched out—Doug came flying in. He lowered his head.

I saw the sunlight reflecting off the top of his shiny helmet. I tried to double over and protect myself with my shoulder, but Neal held me tight. . . .

Books by Bill Wallace

Red Dog
Trapped in Death Cave

Available from ARCHWAY Paperbacks

Beauty
The Biggest Klutz in Fifth Grade
Buffalo Gal
The Christmas Spurs
Danger in Quicksand Swamp
Danger on Panther Peak (original title: *Shadow on the Snow*)
A Dog Called Kitty
Ferret in the Bedroom, Lizards in the Fridge
Snot Stew
Totally Disgusting!

Available from MINSTREL Books

THE BIGGEST KLUTZ IN FIFTH GRADE

BILL WALLACE

A MINSTREL® BOOK

PUBLISHED BY POCKET BOOKS

New York   London   Toronto   Sydney   Tokyo   Singapore

A Minstrel Book published by
POCKET BOOKS, a division of Simon & Schuster Inc.
1230 Avenue of the Americas, New York, NY 10020

Copyright © 1992 by Bill Wallace

Published by arrangement with Holiday House, Inc.

ISBN: 0-671-86970-1

First Minstrel Books printing March 1994

10 9 8 7 6 5 4 3 2 1

A MINSTREL BOOK and colophon are registered trademarks of Simon & Schuster Inc.

Cover art by Dan Burr

Printed in the U.S.A.

To my sister, Keitha Kay Wallace,
who still loves me even though I'm a klutz

CHAPTER

1

It was probably one of the best tackles I ever made. Come to think of it, it *was* the best tackle I ever made.

Neal Moffett, the greatest athlete in Hoover Middle School history, was racing for the goal line. I was the only one between him and a touchdown.

I darted to the left. There was no way I could catch him, but if I could cut the angle down, maybe I could slow him up enough for José or Kent to get back across the field.

I had the angle on him, so he couldn't turn for the goal line. He kept running farther to the side. We were almost to the chain-link fence when he ran upfield.

Then, at the last second, I dove.

It was a beautiful dive. I don't know where the

power or the strength came from. I don't know how I did it. Suddenly I was flying through the air. I was stretched out like an Olympic swimmer doing his best racing dive. Superman would have been impressed with the way I soared across the field.

I hit the ground on my stomach. The air sort of went out of me with a little weak *whoompf*. My left elbow scraped the ground. It burned. Still, I reached as far as I could. And . . .

My left hand struck Neal right above the foot. I couldn't hold his ankle, but the hit was enough. His legs and arms started spinning around like a windmill in a strong storm. Head and body leaning forward, he couldn't keep on his feet. He was going down.

Then I heard a thud. As I slid across Doug's backyard, I saw a big cloud of dust and grass clippings belch up into the blue summer sky.

I did it!

I stopped Neal Moffett.

I was still moving. I was sliding across the yard. The sound of my forehead scraping on the grass and dirt roared like a train inside my head. I could feel the heat.

But just as I started to lift my face up, I slammed into something. There was a loud clanking sound inside my skull. I felt like I'd banged the top of my head into a brick wall. Whatever I hit gave way, but when it did, it took some of my hair with it.

I stopped.

Blinking a couple of times, I tried to shake off the pain. I blinked again.

There was a little piece of wire, with a tuft of brown hair caught in it, almost touching my nose. I opened my right eye wider. A chain-link fence loomed above me. Glistening silver-white, it seemed to stretch forever into the blue sky. I put my hands against the ground and tried to push myself up.

The pain stabbed at the back of my neck like a knife. Desperate, I tried to crawl forward. Something held me in a viselike grip.

The ground felt cool against the left side of my face. The right side of my chin was touching the bottom of the chain-link fence—where the ends of the wires make a little X. I turned my head just a bit, so I could see Neal. Doug and Bobby were helping him up from the ground as Kent Green trotted over with the football.

"Fumble," he chuckled. "Neal fumbled. It's our ball."

Bobby tried to dust Neal off, and Neal knocked his hand away. "Was not!" he growled. "It was a trip. Pat tripped me. It don't count!"

"It was a tackle," José said, coming up next to Kent. "Pat grabbed your ankle with his hand. I saw it! It wasn't a trip, it was a tackle. Our ball!"

I tried to push myself up again. I couldn't move.

When I made that fantastic tackle and went flying across the yard, I hadn't realized how close I was to the chain-link fence. The force of my leap landed me right under the thing.

Well . . . not *clear* under it. My head was the only thing that made it through. Now . . .

I was stuck!

"You guys want to help me?" I called.

Usually when you make a fantastic tackle like I just did, the whole team comes over and slaps you on the back or seat and tells you how great it was. Only, José and Kent were so busy arguing about the fumble, they didn't even notice I wasn't around.

Suddenly there was a bare foot. It was right in front of my face. And an ankle. And long legs.

Hardly able to lift my head, I moved my eyes up those long, shapely legs. From the corner of my right eye, I could see the bottom of a pink bikini bathing suit. Nice hips. A slim, bare waist. The top to the pink bikini—curves in all the right places. Long, blond hair, smooth and shiny as silk. Soft shoulders.

Tiffany Williams smiled down at me.

"Are you all right, Pat?"

I tried to smile back.

"Sure," I lied.

She tilted her head to the side. Those full, beautiful lips of hers gave a little pout.

"Why don't you get up?"

I didn't answer her. How could I tell the most gorgeous, popular, mature girl in the whole school that I tackled Neal Moffett and then slid under her back fence? How could I tell her that I got my neck caught? How could I tell her I was stuck like a pig in the mud? How could I tell Tiffany Williams that I was the biggest klutz in the whole world?

"I'm just resting," I lied. "I'll get up in a second."

I glanced past her to the blue sky. Please let her go back to her air mattress and lie down, I begged. Let her go suntan some more. Just make her go away.

Only Tiffany didn't go away.

"You can't get up, can you? You're stuck."

I closed my eyes. I wanted to die.

"Hey, guys!" Tiffany called in her most feminine voice. "You better come over here. I think Pat's stuck in my fence."

CHAPTER

2

It was bad enough to be trapped under the fence where I couldn't get up. It was even worse for Tiffany to see me like this.

When she yelled at the guys, it took them only half a second to come racing over to her. I doubt that they would even have noticed me if she hadn't said something about it.

Neal was still mad at me for making such a great tackle. He didn't even offer to help. José, Kent, and the others got hold of the fence and tried to lift it off my neck. It was too stiff and new. Every time they pulled on it, the wire cut into the back of my head or the right side of my neck. I tried my best not to wiggle or yell, but I couldn't help it.

Doug and Kent got hold of my ankles while José, Bobby, Larry, and Charlie lifted the wire.

"You'll rip his head off," José finally yelled at them. "Quit pulling."

Doug spun around and raced off for the house. "He's stuck good. I better go get my mom."

Tiffany's feet disappeared from in front of my nose.

"I'll get my mom too," I heard her call.

I felt as helpless as some little sick calf with his head caught in a cattle chute.

Neal just laughed.

"Man, Berry," he scoffed, "you really know how to act cool in front of the girls. This is just like one of your clumsy stunts."

I wanted to get up so much, I could scream. But all I could do was lie there and think about how ridiculous I must look to all my friends. And to Tiffany.

Tiffany Williams kind of grew up before most of the other girls in our class. They liked her because she was smart and nice. Along with being pretty, she was sweet, and that made her popular with the whole class. Then, in fourth grade, she started getting curves. Most of the other girls had long hair and dressed like girls, only . . . well . . . they sort of looked like all the rest of us. Tiffany Williams *looked* like a girl!

That was probably the main reason we'd decided to play football in Doug Loy's backyard. We usually played at Neal's house. Neal had a huge front yard, just right for playing pass football. He also had all the footballs and basketballs and baseball equipment you could imagine. He even had his own set of weights in a separate room at the back of the house.

José said that Neal's dad started training him to be the world's greatest athlete even before he was hatched. (José always said that Neal was hatched instead of born live, like ordinary people.)

When Doug Loy said that Tiffany was working on a suntan, we moved the game over to his yard. Doug and Tiffany were neighbors. The only thing that separated their backyards was the chain-link fence. The first time we played, Doug told us that every day, around noon, Tiffany wore nothing but a hot-pink bikini and stretched out on an air mattress in her pool.

Noon was a bad time for playing football. It was too hot. Doug's yard wasn't much good for football either. There were three pecan trees that sort of messed up our passing game. We also had to watch out for the chain-link fence. All that, plus the fact that Tiffany sometimes had friends over, and we had to deal with a bunch of yucky girls. Doug's yard was probably the worst place in the world for a football game.

Still, hot-pink is an interesting color. . . .

Neal always got to be quarterback. His dad had plans for him to be the quarterback on the high-school team when he got older. Neal's dad wanted him to start practicing now.

I got to be the other quarterback. It wasn't because I was all that good. It was just that I was a lot better at passing than running out for passes. Being a bit on the plump side, I wasn't too fast. Besides, I wore out or got winded before the rest of the gang.

Doug Loy and Bobby Blaton were usually on Neal's team. That's probably because Neal was cool, a super athlete, and the most popular guy in our class. Doug and Bobby, like a lot of the other kids at Hoover, were trying to kiss up to him all the time.

José O'Brien and Kent Green were usually on my team. José was my best friend. Kent, too. José and Kent were fast enough to cover Doug and Bobby. The other reason they were on my team was they didn't like Neal all that much.

Neal was always poking fun at people, especially the guys who didn't go out for football. Maybe making wisecracks or making up really radical nick-

names for people was one of the things that made
Neal so cool. José played trombone in the band.
According to Neal, anybody in the band was a wimp.
He let José know that too. So if Neal picked José to
be on his team, José wouldn't play worth a flip.

Kent didn't play too well when he was on Neal's
team either. Kent was nice looking. Only, he was
kind of on the skinny side. Neal was always calling
him Kent Green the String Bean or saying he was
anorexic. I used to think it was a cool name. I used
to laugh because it fit Kent perfectly. Then I figured
out that Kent was real self-conscious about his
weight. He would eat everything he could get his
hands on, but he never seemed to gain an ounce.
And knowing how much Neal's calling him the
String Bean hurt Kent, it wasn't that funny anymore.

Larry Palmer and Charlie Ratcliff usually didn't
play with us. They didn't live in our neighborhood.
Today, though, they had ridden their bicycles clear
across town.

It hadn't been much of a game. We had played
almost thirty minutes, and the score was still 0–0.
That's probably because none of our pass receivers
were watching the football. I'd overthrown Larry a
couple of times. Then I threw the ball too close to

the fence, and José had scraped his arm. But the rest of my passes had been great. Once I hit Kent in the chest. He dropped it.

Like I said, our pass receivers weren't watching the football.

The guys all stood around talking, trying to figure out some way to get me out of the fence. I heard a door slam from the direction of Tiffany's house. Only, I couldn't move my head enough to see who it was.

Those long, shapely legs appeared in front of me again.

"Mama's on the phone," Tiffany announced. "She'll be out in a second."

Then, next to those legs, another pair of legs appeared. These legs weren't long and shapely. They were long but kind of pudgy. Since I couldn't move my head, all I could do was look up out of the corner of my left eye. I followed the legs to a black bathing suit. There were no curves hidden under the bathing suit. Everything was just straight. A plump tummy sort of loomed over me. Above the tummy, I saw a face.

It was Kristine Plimpton. She glared down at me over her pudgy little tummy, then smiled.

"Got yourself stuck, huh, Pat?"

If I'd been a gopher, I would have burrowed clear into the ground. I hated Kristine Plimpton.

When I was in kindergarten, Mama and Dad made me start dance lessons. Kristine was in my dance class. She used to chase me around and hug me and stuff like that. She even kissed me once. When I was a little-bitty kid, it didn't bother me. In fact, her folks would come over to play cards with my folks sometimes, and Kristine and I would run in the yard or play checkers in the living room.

I used to think Kristine was nice. I was much more grown up now. Kristine hadn't grown up at all! She was also in my class at school. Last year at recess, she still chased me around, wanting me to kiss her. It was enough to make me throw up. When her parents came over to the house, either I'd hide in my room and say I had homework, or I'd go out and play with my friends. She put ice down my back. She hit me. She chased me. I hit her back.

Kristine was a little on the plump side in third grade. Since her name was Plimpton, Neal started out by making fun of her and calling her *Blimp*ton. Then he went on to call her The Blimp-Who-Weighs-a-Ton, and by the end of third grade, he had simply shortened her name to The Blimp.

When Kristine chased or pestered me, I called

her every name I could think of except Blimp or fat—because that's what people called me, and I didn't like it. But no matter how rude I was to her, Kristine Plimpton just kept coming.

Behind her there were two more sets of legs. I could get only short glimpses of them, because Kristine blocked my view like a small mountain. People were talking and laughing.

By the time school started next year, the whole building would know about me getting stuck under Tiffany Williams's fence.

Mrs. Loy finally showed up. She tugged on the fence a couple of times. But when the pain made me yell, she quit.

"He's really stuck." She sighed from someplace above me. "I don't know how we'll ever get him out."

Then the door slammed again from the direction of Tiffany's house. "Is he hurt?" Tiffany's mother shouted. "Is he cut?"

"No," Mrs. Loy called back. "I don't see much blood. But he's really stuck. I don't know how we're ever going to get him out. We better get help!"

That's when I heard the dogs. There was barking—high-pitched, whiny, snippety little yaps from across the yard. The sounds came closer.

I felt my muscles go limp. I sagged into the

ground—a quivering blob that sort of melted away
into the dirt.

It was Butch and Ben, Tiffany's two Pomeranians.
They were the snottiest, nastiest, meanest little
dogs in the whole neighborhood.

As if it wasn't bad enough that I was hurt and
stuck and that Tiffany had a bunch of girls over to go
swimming with her, as if it wasn't bad enough that
Kristine was with them and that the guys had seen
me and that even Mrs. Loy couldn't figure out how
to get me loose and I would probably spend the rest
of my life trapped here—

And as if all that wasn't bad enough, now Butch
and Ben were fixin' to eat my face.

CHAPTER

3

I guess I was lucky.

Mrs. Williams yelled something about the darned dogs slipping out the door. As they bolted across the yard, she kept calling them to come back.

They didn't.

Doug warned the guys that the dogs really would bite.

That helped a lot too.

Kristine grabbed one of them, and Tiffany kicked at the other one when he was less than a foot from my face. It didn't stop him, but it spun him around. He came charging back, though, trying to get at me.

His vicious, short little teeth were almost to my nose when Tiffany reached down and grabbed him. He was so close to me I could smell his stinky, dog-food breath.

Pomeranians have this flufflike tail that flips up over their backs. With their tails up in the air like that, their bare bottoms kind of stick up, making the back ends of them almost as ugly as the little, pug-nose front ends of them.

Tiffany caught the dog by that fluff tail and dragged him back. He kept yapping and barking. His feet dug into the ground as he tried to get loose. Even after Tiffany picked him up in her arms, he was still barking and struggling.

Being saved from those nasty little dogs was the first time I was lucky. The second time was when the firemen showed up.

I could hear the sirens long before the trucks got there. When Mrs. Loy led the firemen around to the backyard, Mrs. Williams recognized one of them.

From the conversation above me, I figured out that she and he had gone to high school together. She wanted to visit with him about old times and see if he had heard from old so-and-so or if he knew where what's-his-name was living now.

I was lucky because the firemen got me out of the fence before the guy who knew Mrs. Williams took time to visit with her.

The men lifted the fence off my neck.

"Lie still until we check for possible neck or spinal injuries," one of them told me.

But before the firemen even got the words out, I had scrambled to my feet.

The men sort of looked me over. They checked my head and my shoulders and the back of my neck where the wire had poked me.

"He's not hurt," one of the firemen said. "Just a few scratches and a couple of shallow puncture wounds."

Kent and José patted me on the shoulders, glad that I was free.

"Should we take him to the doctor?" Mrs. Loy asked.

"Nah," the other fireman answered. "Little hydrogen peroxide ought to fix him up fine. You probably should call his mother and let her know what happened. Have her check to make sure he's had a tetanus shot in the past few years. That's about all."

Jabbering away, Mrs. Williams and Mrs. Loy walked the men toward the front of the house and back to their truck. The girls moved toward the pool. I swear they kept glancing back at me and giggling. The guys all clumped around me, asking if I was hurt or if I was scared and stuff like that. That's when Neal walked up.

"Just like you, Berry," he scoffed. "Always pulling dumb stunts. You're the biggest klutz in the whole state."

I tried to ignore him. "I'm fine," I assured the rest of the guys. Then, trying to move around Neal, I said, "Let's finish the game."

Only, Neal moved between me and where Kent had dropped the football.

"You're always getting hurt. Every year you end up getting stitches or breaking something. Not only are you fat, you're clumsy, too!"

A flash of red clouded my vision. My fists clenched at my side. My teeth ground together so hard, I thought the new filling Dr. Smith put in last week was going to pop out and hit Neal right in the eye. I wish it had. Then I caught myself.

Neal was a fantastic athlete. He lifted weights. He was slim and had muscles. If I hit him, he'd probably beat the tar out of me—right here, in front of the guys . . . and Tiffany Williams. So I made my fists relax. I forced my teeth apart so I could breathe again.

"Let's finish the game," I repeated.

Neal side stepped again, and I couldn't get around him.

"Summer before last, you got your leg broke when you jumped out of a tree. The year before that, you broke your arm falling off your bike—"

"Now wait a minute," José said, scooting between us. "Pat didn't fall off his bike. We were headed to the show and that dumb college kid in the little Honda cut right in front of us. It was his fault, not ours. I was just lucky I didn't get something broke, too."

I moved over, trying to get to the football.

Neal shoved José and cut me off again.

"And last summer you had to have five stitches in your forehead, and—"

José pushed between us. He kind of bumped Neal back with his chest.

"That wasn't Pat's fault, either. He was bending over picking up some dog food that he spilled. His dad didn't see him when he opened the storm door to throw the cat out."

Neal's eyes grew tight as he glared at my friend.

"How about the tree?"

José shrugged.

"Well . . . we got sheets off the water bed for parachutes . . . and . . . well . . . Okay, so jumping out of that tree *was* dumb, but the rest of the stuff . . . well, that wasn't Pat's fault."

Neal practically knocked José out of the way. José started for him. He wasn't scared of Neal like I was. I reached out and caught José's arm.

Neal got right in my face. "You're a klutz, Pat

Berry. I thought your sissy dance lessons were supposed to make you graceful, coordinated."

When he said that, I knew the bit about Twinkletoes Fairy was coming next. Back in fourth grade,
we were playing football at Neal's when I made the
mistake of telling the guys I had to leave so I
wouldn't miss dance class. Ever since, I've wished a
million times that I'd never said that in front of
Neal.

Sure enough, and so loud that not only the guys
but the whole neighborhood could hear, Neal
blurted out:

"Fat Pat Berry, the Twinkletoes Fairy!" Then he
added: "He's the biggest klutz in fifth grade!"

Bobby Blaton patted Neal on the shoulder. "Fat
Pat Berry, the Twinkletoes Fairy," he laughed.
"That's one of the greatest nicknames you ever came
up with, Neal. It fits old Pat like a glove."

Neal laced his thumbs in his belt loops and rocked
back on his heels.

"Yeah, Fat Pat Berry *was* a good name for him,"
he agreed. "But I'm changing it." He cupped a hand
to the side of his mouth. "Hear, ye! Hear, ye!" he
called out like one of the town criers we studied
when we did the unit on British history last year.
"From this day forward, let it be known that Pat

Berry has been given a new name. Fat Pat Berry is now—*The Klutz!*"

Neal had been looking over at the girls, making sure they heard him, and embarrassing me as much as he could. His eyes narrowed when he turned to me. "I bet a thousand dollars you can't get through the summer without breaking something or getting stitches. You're a total klutz!"

It was more than I could take. My fists tightened up again. If only he hadn't said the Fat Pat Berry stuff with Tiffany standing there in her hot-pink bikini. I forced my hands open. I couldn't hit him. He'd kill me. Still, I couldn't let his challenge go. I had to do something.

I took a deep breath.

"Bet I can!"

CHAPTER

4

Mrs. Loy put hydrogen peroxide on my neck and called Mama to check on my tetanus shot. She handed me the phone, and I assured Mama that I was okay. I even got permission to stay awhile longer to finish the football game.

We didn't play football. Instead we sat under one of the pecan trees in Doug's yard. I told Neal that I bet a thousand dollars I *could* go all summer without breaking a bone or having to get stitches.

"It's a bet!" Neal snorted.

"Neither one of you has a thousand dollars," Kent reminded us.

Neal rested his chin in his hand and frowned.

I smiled, trying to look confident and sure of myself.

Neal's lip curled. "All right. I'll bet the weight bench and weights that my dad got me for Christmas. What are you gonna bet?"

I jerked. Weight bench and weights! Man, I thought. What a bet. I'd love . . . no, I'd never lifted weights before. What would I do with a weight bench? But it would be worth it, just for Neal not to have it. Then I frowned. What did I have that could even come close to matching a weight bench and weights?

My bottom lip hurt when I bit down on it.

"All right," I said, swallowing the lump in my throat. "I'll bet . . . I'll bet you my coin collection."

Bobby Blaton tugged at Neal's sleeve. Always the tough guy, Neal knocked his hand away. Bobby tugged at him again.

"What do you want, B.B.?"

B.B. was Neal's nickname for Bobby Blaton. It had kind of a double meaning. First, the letters *B B* were Bobby Blaton's initials. Second, back in third grade Bobby's dad got him a BB gun for his birthday. One day somebody bet him he couldn't hit a cop car that was driving by. Nobody could believe he really did it. The BB gun got stuck in his dad's closet. Bobby got stuck with the name B.B. probably forever.

Bobby shrugged.

"Neal, your dad would kill you if you gave something as expensive as a weight bench away."

Neal's shoulders kind of sagged.

Kent leaned forward. From the corner of my eye, I could see him shake his head.

"Your mom would kill you, too," he said, "if you lost your coin collection."

I nodded.

Neal sat up straight again.

"All right. I'll bet my bicycle."

"Your bike's a piece of junk," José said.

"Well, so's Pat's," B.B. said, jumping in.

We thought about it for a second, and then everybody kind of slumped. Resting our chins in our hands, we sat for a long while, buried in thought.

José O'Brien was probably thinking the hardest. At least he looked like he was. José was kind of a mixed-up kid. I mean, with a name like José O'Brien . . . His dad was a redheaded Irishman. José said he'd gotten his temper from his dad. His mother was Mexican. She'd given him her temper, too. She'd also given him the name José, because that was her father's name. José had his mother's dark complexion and dark hair. The dark hair covered his head like a thick blanket. He had dark, dark eyebrows, too. In fact, they were so thick and dark and big, they sort of grew together in the middle of his forehead. José seemed to have one giant eyebrow that stretched clear across his face. When he was buried in thought, his eyebrow formed a deep V, kind of like an arrow pointing down at his nose.

Finally the eyebrow arched.

"I got it. Since neither of you has any money, and neither of you has anything your parents will let you bet or anything worth betting, why not *do* something?"

Neal frowned and looked at José out of one eye.

"Like what?"

José shrugged.

"I don't know. Maybe you each have to do something you really don't want to do."

"Yeah," B.B. chimed in. "Like throw rocks at a cop car or jump off the Placer Tower."

Everybody turned on Bobby and sneered. B.B. wasn't too bright.

He gave a little shrug.

"Well, somethin' like that anyway."

José's eyebrow dipped again.

"No. It can't be anything dangerous. We can't do something where somebody gets hurt or killed. It's gotta be somethin' bad but not stupid."

We all slumped forward and thought some more.

Charlie Ratcliff gave a little jerk. His eyes flashed wide.

"I got it." His voice was changing, and he squealed instead of yelling. He cleared his throat and glanced around to make sure the girls swimming in Tiffany's pool hadn't heard. Then, more softly, he repeated. "I got it. The first day of school—out in the hall, when we're changing classes, and loud enough for the whole building to hear—the loser has to call Coach Kruger 'Freddie'!"

Our blood ran cold. We gasped. We slapped our hands over our mouths.

It had been common knowledge in our town for years that you simply didn't call Coach Kruger "Freddie." Some of the older guys, like in high school, said that it all started when the movie *Nightmare on Elm Street* first came out. The villain was named Freddie Kruger, so some of the guys started calling Coach Kruger "Freddie." (Come to think of it, he looked a lot like Freddie Kruger.)

Nobody knew what Coach Kruger's first name really was. Everybody called him Coach, because he used to coach baseball. But one thing we knew for sure, his first name *wasn't* Freddie.

When a new kid named Herman Hawthorne from

a little town in Oklahoma called Chickasha moved in last year, some of the eighth graders convinced him that Coach liked the guys in school to call him by his first name. Herman didn't know the guys were putting him on, so he went right up to Coach Kruger and said, "Freddie, I'd like to try out for the football team. Could you tell me when practice starts?"

Coach Kruger was the assistant principal—the guy who took care of discipline at Hoover Middle School. He didn't like being called Freddie, but he *did* like his job.

Poor Herman spent the whole first week of school in detention hall.

When Coach got to stick somebody in detention for a few days, he went around for a whole week in a good mood. If Coach Kruger so much as heard someone say "There goes Freddie Kruger," the rest of that kid's days at Hoover Middle School would be *total torture*.

A little smile tugged at the corners of my mouth with the thought of Charlie's suggestion. It sounded like the perfect thing for Neal Moffett.

"I like it!" I said, trying not to smile too much.

Neal shook his head so hard, it looked like there was an earthquake inside his body.

"No way, man. Dad wants me on the football team. I can't be on the team if Freddie's got me in detention all the time. No way."

We all sat quietly for a long time. Finally Larry Palmer cleared his throat.

"Maybe the first day of school, the loser would have to streak through the hall in his underwear."

Everybody shook his head.

"Maybe the loser could kiss a pig or somethin'," Kent suggested.

I didn't like the sudden smile that swept across Neal Moffett's face. In the blink of an eye, he was on his feet. He ran to the chain-link fence and beckoned to Tiffany.

I didn't like that either.

Tiffany came to the fence, and Neal talked with her a second. Then Tiffany went back to the pool and whispered something to Kristine, who followed her back to the fence. Both girls started whispering with Neal.

Now I was really getting nervous.

Cautiously I got to my feet and started over. The rest of the guys followed.

"Would you let me or Pat walk you to school the first day of class next year?" Neal asked Kristine.

Kristine looked at Neal, then at me. She seemed to study me a moment. She seemed suspicious.

"Why?"

Neal shrugged. "Carry your books for you or somethin'."

"We don't have books the first day of school." Kristine frowned.

Neal smiled. "Well then, just to have somebody to walk with."

My heart pounded in my throat. Kristine shrugged.

"Yeah." She smiled. "I guess. If one of you asked me."

Neal glanced back at me.

"And if one of us wanted to kiss you . . . would you let him?"

Tiffany giggled. Kristine looked at me and winked.

My legs felt like Jell-O.

"I guess. If one of you tried to kiss me, I might let you."

There was a sinister grin on Neal's face.

"And if there were other people around, would you still let one of us kiss you?"

"Like what other people?"

"Like the whole school. You know how we all hang around out in front before the bell rings?"

She folded her arms and rested them on her pudgy tummy. "Just what's going on?"

Neal explained the bet. As he did, Kristine kept watching me. I guess she could see me fidgeting. I jumped from one foot to the other. I wiggled. I shuddered.

When Neal was through explaining the bet *and* reminding her that she'd been trying to catch me at recess ever since second grade, he asked again:

"Well, would you?"

Kristine shrugged again.

"Sure."

"You got to swear. You got to swear on your grandmother's grave that if Pat or I try to kiss you, you'll let us."

Kristine frowned. "Both my grandmothers are still alive. They don't have a grave."

"Well, when they die," Neal insisted. "You got to swear on their graves that no matter what, if Pat or I walk you to school the first day of class and want to kiss you—you'll do it."

Kristine kind of frowned at Neal. Then she studied me a moment. Her dark eyes seemed to twinkle over those pudgy little cheeks of hers.

"Okay," she said finally. "I swear!"

My heart sank clear down to the bottoms of my grungy tennis shoes. I couldn't look her in the eye. I glanced at the ground, staring at the bottom of the fence. I wished I was still caught under the thing. I wished I was still trapped and dying. I wished Butch and Ben had eaten my face. I would rather be dead than . . .

than . . . have to kiss . . .

The Blimp.

CHAPTER

5

"I can't believe I was stupid enough to bet with Neal. Of all the dumb, idiotic, ignorant . . ." I shook my head. "Not only am I the biggest klutz in school, now I'm the biggest, stupidest klutz in the whole town. It's not fair!"

José was walking on one side of me, Kent on the other. We were walking home together, our arms wrapped around each other's shoulders. I don't know whether they were hanging on to me offering their support, or whether I was hanging on to them to keep from falling down on the ground and bawling.

"It's not fair!" I pleaded again.

Kent patted me on the shoulder.

"I messed up when I said something about kissin' a pig. Never figured Neal would get the idea for kissing *The Blimp* from that. But the bet's as fair as we could make it. You can do it, Pat. All you got to do is be careful. Don't get hurt."

"But if I do . . ."

I made a gulping sound when I swallowed.

"You won't," José insisted. "We're gonna help you. My sister Terry has a balance beam out in the backyard. We can lower the thing so if you fall off, you won't get hurt. We'll work on your balance and coordination."

"We got to work on your weight, too." Kent pinched the little roll of fat that stuck out at the top of my jeans.

"Quit!" I yelped, knocking his hand away.

"You are . . . well, Pat, you're a little on the plump side. You're more liable to trip over stuff if you can't see your feet because of your stomach."

"Thanks a lot, *pal!*"

Kent shrugged. "Sorry, but . . ."

I glanced at the blue sky.

"It's not fair" was all I could say.

Kent and José held me up between them.

"I can't understand why Neal is so popular," José said. "I mean . . . just because he's a good athlete. If the other guys at school knew him as well as we do, they'd see what a jerk he is." He shook his head. "I mean, if you have so much as one stitch for a split lip or one little broken pinkie, you've had it. Man, that's rough."

"Yeah," Kent agreed. "And Doug was a regular snot, too. Right as we were leaving, he up and says, 'Not just a little peck on the cheek—a real kiss, on the lips, puttin' your arms around her and having to kiss her for a whole ten seconds, on the lips.' . . ."

My stomach rolled over at the thought.

The disgust oozed from Kent's voice. "How come Neal gets to make all the rules? We need to make up some rules, too."

"Yeah," José said. "Tonight we need to figure out some rules to help Pat out."

We stood at the back steps of my house for a long time. I guess I was afraid that if they let go of my shoulders, I would crumple up and collapse.

"I'm always falling down." I sighed.

José hugged my shoulder. "We all do. We play football or stuff, where you either fall down or get knocked down. You just got to be careful. *Real care-ful!*"

Kent shook my arm.

"You're gonna make it, Pat. And if you start get-ting depressed or worried, just think about Neal Moffett. Think about him puckering up and The

Blimp's big fat lips coming at *him* and . . . well, that ought to make you feel better."

Kent had to go help his dad mow the lawn. José had to get home, too. They left me there, holding the handrail by my back steps with both hands.

That night, when I fed Chomps, I fixed his food far from the back door. Dad was always getting mad at Mootz, our dumb cat. I made sure I was out of the way, so if he flung the door open to throw the cat out, the door wouldn't clunk me in the head, like last year.

I didn't wrestle with Chomps or get him to chase me around the backyard, either. Sometimes when we got to playing too rough, he'd nip at me. He never hurt me, but even so, I was going to be extra careful from now on.

When I took my shower, I put the bath mat—the little rubber thing with the suction cups on the bottom—on the floor of the shower stall. I had never used it before, and I had to practically stand on my head in the bathroom closet, hunting for the dumb thing. It'd be my luck to slip and break my thumb if I didn't find it.

Before I went to bed that night, I gathered up the extra pillows from the hall closet. I was probably four the last time I fell out of bed. Just the same, I stacked the extra pillows around my bed before crawling under the sheets.

I didn't go to sleep. I couldn't. When I closed my eyes, I could see Kristine Plimpton's pudgy face. I guess when you're fat, you want skinny girls to notice you. You don't want somebody fat like yourself to be the only one who's interested.

My eyes popped open, so I flopped on my back and pulled the pillow over my face. That didn't help, either. Now I could see Neal. The only way Neal could feel cool was by putting other people down. Guys in the band were wimps. Guys who made good grades were nerds. Guys who wouldn't play football with us were dweebs. And guys who took dance lessons—me being the only one Neal could find in the whole school—guys who danced were twinkletoes fairies.

That's just the way Neal was. That's what made him popular. Why—I never could figure.

I had to get some sleep. I forced my eyes shut.

And in that twilight that comes right before sleep, I saw the whole thing. . . .

Everybody in school was there when I walked Kristine to the front steps on the first day of classes.

My teachers, all the guys, all the girls in Hoover Middle School stood waiting for the bell.

Kristine and I stopped at the steps. I turned. I looked at Kristine. I saw her brown eyes twinkling at me over the puffs of her pudgy cheeks. I saw her fat lips pucker up. Those lips were coming right for me.

Suddenly I was sitting straight up in bed. Damp from a cold sweat, I felt my stomach roll and tumble and churn. I wrapped a pillow over my tummy.

I was gonna throw up.

CHAPTER

6

José's dark eyebrow dipped so low, it almost touched the bridge of his nose. He held my arm up to inspect it in the noonday light.

"Where'd you get that bruise?"

I tried to pull my arm away.

"What bruise?"

He poked the blue spot with a finger. "This one. Right here on your arm."

"Oh, that bruise." I tried to sound surprised. "I sort of tripped over some pillows I had on the floor. I had to get up and go to the bathroom, and I . . . well, I sort of bumped into the dresser."

"What were you doing with pillows on the floor?"

I brushed his question away with a wave of my hand. "Forget it. I got the pillows picked up. It won't happen again."

José glared at me. "Soon as we leave here, we're going to your house and check stuff out." He shoved the gate open, and we went to join Neal, Doug, and B.B. under the pecan tree. Kent got there right after we did. Larry and Charlie showed up about ten minutes later.

Kent and José wanted to add some rules to our little challenge. They needed to get some paper so we could write stuff down and keep track of all that was being said.

Doug went into the house to get his notebook from last year's science class. We were sitting in a circle, visiting with each other and laughing, when Doug came back. Suddenly he stopped—froze in his tracks—like a bird dog on point.

We all turned toward Tiffany's house, knowing that her coming out to the pool was the only reason Doug would have stopped so quickly. Tiffany had on the hot-pink bikini again. We watched her and kind of held our breath as she walked and wiggled to the pool. Everybody sat up real straight when she bent down to pick up her air mattress. I sucked my stomach in. She tossed the mattress into the pool. She reached out one long, shapely leg to test the water. There wasn't a sound from any of us. Tiffany jumped in the water. We craned our necks so we could see. She crawled up on the mattress and stretched out on her stomach. We sighed.

Doug finally came across the yard and sat down next to Neal. He flipped through his pages of science notes until he came to a blank page.

"Okay," he said, holding the pencil ready. "What are these rules you and Kent want to add?"

José put his hand against the side of his face. He pushed his head around so he was looking at the guys instead of staring wistfully at Tiffany's hot-pink bikini.

"Ah . . . rules? What rules?"

Everybody laughed.

José smiled. "Okay. Rules. First off, Neal can't do anything to Pat."

Doug didn't write anything. "What do you mean?"

"I mean he can't bash him with a baseball bat or poke a stick in his bicycle spokes while we're riding down the street or anything like that."

"Oh, I get it," Larry Palmer said, trying to help explain. "You mean Neal can't do anything on purpose, like trying to break Pat's leg or make him get hurt."

José nodded. "That's right. If Pat gets hurt, it's got to be on his own—with no help from Neal."

Doug wrote it down.

"And no new, weird games," Kent said. "We got to do the stuff we usually do during the summer."

"Yeah," José jumped in. "And no dares, either. Nothing like daring him to swing on the flagpole at the First National Bank or ride his bike across the freeway."

"And he can't get any of the high-school guys to hurt Pat, either," Kent added.

Neal's mouth flopped open.

"Now how would I do that?"

Kent folded his arms and looked at him out of one eye. "You know. Promise them you'd fix 'em up on a date with your sister Becky if they did something to Pat. Like try to hit him with their car or beat him up or stuff."

"That's stupid," Neal scoffed.

Larry Palmer tugged on his earlobe. "It's not that stupid. Becky *was* homecoming queen last year. She's popular and cute, too. A lot of guys want a date with her."

"Yeah," Charlie Ratcliff agreed. "Remember last summer when we camped out under the picnic table in your backyard? Remember how four different guys climbed over the fence and tried to peek in her window? Some of those guys would do *anything* you told 'em if they thought you could get your sister to go out with them."

Neal slumped. Then he straightened up.

"But what if Pat pulls his bike out in front of somebody in high school that I don't even know? Or that other rule about me not doing anything to Pat? When we play football, what am I supposed to do, just stand there and watch him make touchdowns? You mean I can't even tackle him?"

Doug had stopped writing.

"Yeah, and that one about no new games," he said, chewing thoughtfully on his eraser. "We're always coming up with new things to do. What if somebody comes up with something really fun? We can't do it?"

"I think if Pat gets his eye poked out, that ought to count, too." Bobby sniffed.

Everybody stopped talking and arguing. We kind of gaped at him. He sniffed again. (Along with being a little slow, B.B. had allergies, too.)

"Well," he said finally, when nobody responded. "I mean, if he gets his eye poked out . . . well, it ain't a broke bone or stitches . . . but . . . it's a bad hurt. It ought to count." Sniff.

Doug sighed. "What about the new games? You mean we can't do anything new or different?"

Kent chewed on his fingernail. José's eyebrow

dipped low over his nose. Larry and Charlie rested their chins in their hands.

It took us over two hours to come up with all the rules. We really weren't talking or arguing all that time. Doug had to go in the house to sharpen his pencil once. When he came out, he froze on that bird-dog point again. We got up on our knees so we could see into Tiffany Williams's pool. She had undone the strap to the top of her hot-pink bikini. She was lying on her stomach, with nothing showing but bare skin and her bikini bottom. When Larry saw her, he fell backward. He plopped flat on his back like he'd fainted or something. The rest of us just ignored him. We stood up for a better look.

Like I said, we didn't spend the whole two hours talking and arguing. For about thirty minutes, all eight of us kind of leaned against the pecan tree and stared into the Williams's yard.

Finally Tiffany hooked the top of her bikini. How she did it without moving a half inch off the air mattress nobody knew. It was a total disappointment. When she went inside, we got back to work. Doug did a lot of erasing and marking out in his science notebook. But at long last we had it done.

"I think me and Bobby ought to be judges," Doug said.

José shook his head. "No way, man. I think Kent and me ought to be judges."

Neal laughed. "You two always side with Pat."

We finally agreed on Charlie and Larry. Both were on the football team with Neal, but they were honest. In fact, they were probably the most honest guys at Hoover.

"Here you go," Doug said when he was through making the second copy. He ripped a sheet from the book and handed it to me. "All done."

José and Kent leaned over my shoulder as I read:

1. Stitches (even one), broken bones, cut-off fingers or toes, and/or poked-out eyes between now and the first day of school—COUNT!

2. Broken nose or sprains *DON'T COUNT!*

3. Pat must report all injuries to his parents and go to the doctor if they tell him to.

4. Vacations COUNT! (When Pat comes back from vacation, he has to strip in the tunnel under the highway so we can check if he got any stitches.)

5. Neal (or friends) can't hurt Pat ON PURPOSE!

6. If Pat gets hurt by a high-school kid who is dating or wants to date Becky, it DOESN'T COUNT!

7. New games are permitted as long as they're something that won't get us killed and as long

as they're something ALL of us can do together.

8. Pat has to join in on stuff. If we all play or do
   something, Pat has to do it, too.
9. Larry Palmer and Charlie Ratcliff will be the
   FINAL JUDGES!

I folded the piece of notebook paper and started
to put it in my pocket. José pulled it away from me
and stuck it in his own pocket.

"I need to study this a little more. Come on.
We're going to your house."

He got up and helped me to my feet. Charlie and
Larry got on their bikes and headed back across
town. Doug, B.B., and Neal stayed under the pecan
tree.

"Why are we going to my house?" I asked about
halfway down the block.

"Gonna do a safety inspection," José told me.

"Huh?"

"You know," he explained. "Check out your
room, the house. See if there's stuff you could get
hurt on. Wires stretched across the floor, loose carpet, unsafe ladders."

All I could do was shake my head.

"I was talking to my dad last night," Kent said on
my other side. "He's the assistant coach on the high-
school football team. He says that people are less

likely to get hurt if they're in good shape. Mom says losing weight is the best way. Daddy says conditioning is."

"What kind of conditioning?" I asked.

"Lifting weights. Running. Sit-ups. He said that the high-school weight room is open in the mornings during summer. We're gonna start you exercising there tomorrow."

"I'll help you with your weight," José added. "From now on, you don't get to eat *nothin'* unless I say it's okay. Not so much as one candy bar, one pack of potato chips."

His eyebrow was straight. No arch, no dip—just a straight, dark line across his brow.

Suddenly, as we walked to my house, I felt that Kent and José were more like bodyguards than friends. They made me stop at every single corner. They looked both ways, then kept me between them as we crossed.

At my house José carefully opened the front door for me. Kent took my elbow and tried to help me up the stairs.

I jerked my arm away and glared at him.

With these guys hovering over me like a couple of mother hens all summer, I'd be nuts by August.

CHAPTER

7

I curled up on my bed with a comic book while Kent and José rattled around the house.

I could hear them talking as they moved from room to room. Every once in a while something would go *bonk* or *rattle*. I just hoped they weren't tearing up anything that would get me in trouble with Mama and Dad when they got home.

A long time passed when I didn't hear anything from them. Finally they came back to my room. Kent checked around the bed. He even felt around the sides.

"These corners sure are sharp," he commented.

I gave a little snort.

"This has got to go," José said.

I peeked over the top of my comic.

"My Nintendo?"

He shook his head. "Not the game, just all these cords and junk you got laying here." He opened the little drawer on the stand under my TV. He stuffed the wires inside and closed it. "One control knob. That's all you need. Got to keep the rest of those wires in the drawer. You might trip on them."

After they finished inspecting my room, they came to my bed and sat down, one on either side of me.

"Everything looks pretty good," José said. "Is there any way you could change rooms with your little sister? I'd feel a lot better if your room was downstairs. Those steps are pretty steep. Think your folks would let you trade?"

"No."

"Found a phone cord stretched across the doorway to the kitchen," Kent said. "We put it under the carpet."

"We got some of that gray tape out of your dad's workroom." José smiled. "We taped down the throw rug in the hall. You could slip on that thing."

"Your dad doesn't let you use any of his power tools in his shop, does he?" Kent wondered.

I shook my head.

"Good. No saws or drills or anything like that. No helping your dad in his shop until school starts."

"Stay off the ladder next to the garage, too," José said. "No climbing on the roof. Basketball gets stuck, call Kent or me. We'll get it down for you."

My eyes rolled.

"We'll be with you, Pat. Anytime you need us, just yell," José assured me. "I'll come over whenever my mom and dad let me. I'll help you watch what you eat."

"We'll take care of you, Pat," Kent promised. "I'll work out with you in the weight room." He reached over and folded down the corner of my comic. "Oh, by the way," he said, making me look at him, "we checked your refrigerator, too. Your mom sure has a lot of junk food. I'm gonna make a list and bring it to you. Next time she goes to the store, have her pick up the stuff. It'll help. And when José can't come over, I'll invite myself to supper so I can help you stay on your diet."

Both of them patted me on the back.

"We're with you all the way, man! Anything you need. We'll watch out for you and . . ."

I crunched the comic book in my lap. Then I picked it up and slung it across the room.

Startled, they both shut up.

"Next thing I know," I roared, "you guys won't even let me go to the bathroom by myself."

They frowned and just looked at me.

"What does that mean?" José's eyebrow dipped to his nose.

"It means you guys are gonna drive me crazy!" I snapped, glaring at José. "You're gonna come over and watch everything I eat. You're gonna get my basketball off the roof." I turned on Kent. "You're gonna make a list of food for my mom. You're gonna make me lift weights and do sit-ups." I jerked my head, turning back to José. "You're gonna open doors for me, to make sure nobody's coming out." Then to Kent: "And you're gonna grab my arm like some Boy Scout helping a little old lady across the street and help me up the steps *to my own house*! You guys are gonna drive me *nuts*!"

Looking a little puzzled, they sat there a moment. Finally José smiled. He reached over and yanked the pillow from under my shoulders. My head gave a little clunk when it bounced off the headboard.

Then José slugged me with the pillow.

"Pat's sweet on Kristine!" he yelped.

"Am not!"

"He wants to get hurt this summer so he can kiss her."

"Do not!"

I tried to grab the pillow away from him. I missed, and he pounded me again.

"Are too."

"Am *not*, you idiot!"

"Yeah you are. That's why you don't want Kent and me helping you. You want to lose the bet. You want to give Kristine *Blimp*ton a big, sloppy kiss— right on the lips."

He laughed and slugged me again. Then he started singing, "Pat loves The Blimp. Pat loves The Blimp."

I pounced on him. I was going to get that pillow and pound him to death with the thing. We wrestled on the bed, flopping and grabbing and tumbling over each other. Finally José was laughing so hard, I got the pillow. I bounced it on his head a couple of times.

Then, from the corner of my eye, I saw Kent. He made a flying leap across my bed. All three of us went tumbling to the floor. Laughing and giggling and rolling around, we finally came to rest against the door to my room. We were panting and out of breath from all the fun and the sudden wrestling match. José nudged me with his elbow and tugged one last time on the pillow.

"You really don't want to have to kiss The Blimp, do you, Pat?"

I was kind of gasping for air, so all I did was shake my head.

"You'd a lot rather Neal Moffett kissed her," he puffed, "right?"

I nodded.

"Okay, then." He patted my knee. "Let Kent and me help watch out for you."

I nodded.

"Okay," I huffed. "I *do* need to lose some weight. And working out at the weight room probably wouldn't hurt me, either." I sucked in another deep breath. "But this junk about helping me across streets . . ."

I slugged José and Kent with my pillow.

"That stuff's overdoing it!"

They threw up their hands. Then they tried to grab the pillow. I wrapped my arms around it and clutched it to my stomach.

"Okay," they agreed, still laughing. "We promise we won't overdo it."

It was about suppertime, so I walked my friends downstairs. Before they turned to go their separate ways, both looked back at me and waved.

"Be careful, Pat!"

For the next three months, every time they left me, that's the last thing they said:

"Be careful, Pat!"

I thought I'd have a few minutes of peace and quiet before Mama and Dad got home. I went to my room and got one of the books I'd checked out at the library. I had just opened it when the phone rang.

Being careful on the stairs, I trotted down to answer it.

"Hello?"

"Pat?" It was José.

"Yeah, José. It's me. What?"

"I forgot to tell you something, Pat."

"What?"

"Neal."

"What about Neal?"

"You got to watch him, Pat." His voice was very serious. "Along with being a smart mouth and thinking he's really hot stuff, Neal Moffett's also the biggest sneak in school. You can't trust him for a minute, Pat. And you can bet money he'll try to come up with something."

CHAPTER

8

The last two weeks of June went pretty smoothly. We played football at Doug Loy's. Except for trying to rip my arm off a couple of times when he tackled me, Neal really didn't try anything.

We spent those two weeks playing football and drooling over the fence at Tiffany and her hot-pink bikini. Sometimes Kristine and the other girls would show up to swim. I was always afraid Kristine would say something about our kiss or pop off in front of Tiffany about how she could hardly wait for me to walk her to school.

She never did.

I worried about it though until the first of July. Then I heard that Kristine's parents had sent her to a camp way up in Maine. She'd be there the rest of the summer. She wouldn't be back until right before school started.

Now I could breathe a little easier.

I could breathe a little easier because I didn't have to worry about Kristine embarrassing me in front of my friends. I could also breathe better because of Kent and José.

Every Monday, Wednesday, and Friday mornings, regular as the bells in the Catholic church steeple, Kent and José came by at nine o'clock to pick me up. We walked over to the high-school weight room. Kent's dad, who along with being assistant football coach was in charge of the weight program, worked with us the first two or three days. He showed us what weights to use and how to handle the machines. He showed us the right way to do stuff—how to lift, and what not to do on certain machines.

On the bench press we started out lifting nothing but the bar. Each week we added five pounds. We worked on the vertical sit-up machine, the leg press, and the leg-lift machine. I could do more on the leg machines than either Kent or José. They couldn't figure it out. I couldn't either. Both of them could run circles around me, so we always figured their legs were a lot stronger. Finally, when we asked Kent's dad about it, he reached over and patted my tummy. "Pat's been carrying around a lot more weight than you guys for years. His legs are stronger from carrying the weight, but he's also slower because he has to lug all that fat around." He pinched one of the rolls of fat on my side. "But we're gonna take care of that."

After about an hour and a half in the weight room, we went over to the high-school stadium. There was a track that circled the football field. It looked like asphalt, but it was a lot softer on the feet. It had yellow-and-red-striped lanes. Four laps was a mile, so we circled the thing eight times. The first morning, I didn't even make it around once before I had to stop and walk. After two weeks I could finish only two laps without having to walk. Even on those two laps, Kent and José had to jog slow so I could keep up.

After lifting weights and jogging around the track, we went back home and got our bicycles. We rode down to McDonald's and ate lunch.

I hated eating there with Kent and José. We were hot and tired and *hungry* after our workouts. Kent, always trying to gain some weight, would order two Big Macs or a nine-piece Chicken McNuggets, large fries, and a shake. José had either a McBLT and large fries or a Big Mac and fries.

I got a salad or one of those McLean burgers. No fries. No shake. No pop. Just water.

On Tuesdays and Thursdays, we either slept in or did our various chores around the house. After lunch we met at the public swimming pool and played there most of the afternoon.

"There's nothing in the rules about drowning!" José said the first day. "If you don't dive off the diving board or run around the pool, you probably won't break anything or bust your lip or head. If you drown, it don't count, so that's okay."

It really made me feel good when my friend told me it was okay to drown, just as long as I didn't break any bones or get stitches.

Kent brought the list of stuff for Mama to get at the grocery store. It was mostly celery and carrots and lots of fruit. I hated celery more than I hated going with Kent and José to McDonald's.

One day José brought me a pair of big plastic safety goggles and his shin guards from soccer. He made me promise to wear them whenever I mowed the lawn.

The goggles were always fogging up so I couldn't see. It took me twice as long to mow the lawn as it usually did—but I wore the dumb things, just like I promised I would.

With Kristine away at camp, I could relax a little bit at the football games. Of course, as word of Tiffany Williams's hot-pink bikini spread, the games got a little more complicated. When we first started, there had been just six of us. Neal Moffett, Doug Loy, and Bobby Blaton were on one team. José O'Brien, Kent Green, and I were on the other. Then Larry Palmer and Charlie Ratcliff joined us, and before long Rick Davis and Jimmy Jones rode their bikes over. Next Curt Johnson, who lived way out in the country, talked his dad into bringing him to town on his way to work. He hung around at Gary Pitts's house from eight in the morning until noon. Then he and Gary walked over to join us.

By the first week of July, there were twelve of us trying to play football in Doug Loy's tiny backyard.

On the afternoon of July Fourth, Rick Davis brought over some M-80s, although shooting off fireworks was illegal. As soon as Tiffany rolled over on her stomach, we called time-out. Quiet as we could be, we crept to the chain-link fence.

Our plan was that Rick would light a firecracker and toss it near the pool. When it exploded, Tiffany would jump up to see what the bang was. She'd be so startled or scared by the sudden unexpected noise, she'd forget to resnap her bikini top.

We held our hands over our mouths to keep her from hearing our giggles as Rick lit the thing and tossed it. The fuse hissed. Then there was a silent, *very* disappointing puff of smoke.

A dud!

Rick lit a second firecracker. We shifted from one foot to the other. Again we held our hands over our mouths. Any sound might tip Tiffany off. There wasn't a whisper.

Sizzle . . . sizzle . . .

Bang!

Our eyes opened wide. Our hearts raced.

Tiffany lifted her head from the mattress. Calmly she laid her cheek down on the pillow and looked at the line of boys hanging over her back fence. Without lifting anything but her head, without rising a fraction of an inch from her floating mattress, Tiffany Williams just smiled at us.

Our shoulders drooped. Our chins, along with our hopes, dropped clear down to our knees.

We went back to the football game.

With twelve of us trying to play, it was so crowded in Doug Loy's backyard, we could barely move without somebody running into a pecan tree, hitting the chain-link fence, or tripping over another player.

Still, the games were fun.

Then—tragedy struck.

Tiffany Williams, hot-pink bikini and all, flew off to Seattle to visit her grandparents.

CHAPTER

9

With Tiffany Williams visiting her grandparents for the summer, I expected our football games to come to a screeching halt. I knew we wouldn't give up football, but I at least figured there would only be the original six of us playing.

Wrong!

The game simply moved from the once interesting scenery of Doug Loy's tiny backyard to the wide-open spaces of Neal Moffett's front yard. We also moved the time up. It was better to play in the morning during the cool part of the day.

With football in the mornings, I figured I could get out of going to the weight room.

Wrong again!

Kent talked his dad into letting him have the key in the afternoons. After we finished lunch at Mc-

Donald's, José, Kent, and I trotted off to the high-school weight room, regular as clockwork.

The football games got even bigger. By the middle of July, Herb Scott, Denny Perrin, Pepper Young, and Ben Steward had joined us. Now there were sixteen guys showing up for every game.

Somehow word had gotten out about the bet.

Probably most of the guys were hanging around hoping I'd get hurt. Fat Pat Berry, the Twinkletoes Fairy (now known as The Klutz), kissing The Blimp would make earthshaking news at Hoover Middle School.

I think a few of the other guys secretly hoped I'd make it through the summer. If they said anything to me or sort of cheered me on, they might get on Neal's bad side, though. So they had to keep it quiet. If you got on Neal Moffett's bad side, it was hard to be cool. He might even give you one of his famous nicknames. All of a sudden everybody in school would be calling you fat, or skinny, or dopey, or dumb, or dirty.

Still, Herb Scott whispered to me one morning, after I ducked one of Neal's most vicious tackles, "Glad he missed. Sure hope you can keep dodging. Sure would like to see Neal kiss The Blimp." Then he put his finger to his lips and glanced over his shoulder to make sure nobody had heard. "Shhh. Don't tell anybody I said that."

With so many guys playing, we had some great games. Football, swimming, talking, and seeing my friends—it was neat.

Mama had to buy me some new shirts. The old ones were loose around my stomach, but they were getting too tight around the chest and shoulders. Dad said something one evening about how I had muscles. It made me feel good that he'd noticed. I even got to the point where I could jog the whole two miles at the track without having to stop. Kent and José still had to run slow so I could keep up with them, but I could go all eight laps.

Even Neal, except for some rough tackles, never tried to hurt me or do anything sneaky.

Finally Tiffany Williams came back from visiting her grandparents in Seattle.

It was turning out to be a pretty good summer after all. Not just pretty good. It was turning into a *great summer*.

Then, around the first of August, things started happening.

CHAPTER

10

Football's dangerous. So are girls.

Tiffany got a new bikini when she was in Seattle. It was yellow instead of hot pink. But the yellow bikini not only showed off her cute figure, it also showed off her beautiful bronze skin. And . . . with the yellow bikini, there was even *more* skin than with the pink one.

The day we heard Tiffany was back in town, our football games returned to Doug's yard. Jimmy Jones was running his pass pattern and trying to watch Tiffany climb onto the air mattress. He crashed into a pecan tree headfirst. He ended up spread-eagled on the ground, knocked out cold as a mackerel.

He didn't get cut or anything, but he was out for a long time. It scared us.

He finally woke up, but only after his mom got

there and the emergency crew came. One of the firemen kept yelling at us to stand back. The other broke open a little vial of stuff and stuck it under Jimmy's nose. He started coughing and sputtering. He sat up, looking around to see where he was.

When his mother carried him to the car, we all clumped around and followed. As they drove off to the doctor's office, Mrs. Loy announced that there would be *no more football games* in her backyard. The yard was just too small and there were simply too many boys!

So we went back to playing football at Neal's house. We packed sack lunches, and after the game, at exactly twelve o'clock, we sat around under one of Doug Loy's pecan trees and ate.

We had the best of both worlds. We still got to play football, *and* over lunch, we got to watch Tiffany Williams.

One morning Denny Perrin wore track shoes.

Guys don't wear track shoes to play football. Track shoes have little, sharp spikes on the bottoms. The spikes make them great for gripping a track and running, but they're too sharp and dangerous for sports. Coaches won't let football players or even soccer players use those sharp metal spikes.

No one noticed them. Not until Neal and Doug

tackled me. I was on the ground, trying to get up, when Denny came running over. Hopping on one foot, he started pawing at me with the other.

I saw those bright, shiny, sharp spikes coming right for my cheek. I rolled to the side as fast as I could. Denny hopped after me.

He kept jumping on one foot and pawing the ground with the other. I still don't know how I managed to stay inches from his reach.

Suddenly Kent was there. He pushed Denny back and helped me up. Then José was there. He looked at the cleats on Denny's shoes. He looked at me. Then I guess his Irish/Spanish temper got the best of him.

He flew into Denny like a buzz saw. He was hitting, swinging, kicking—everything to beat Denny Perrin to a pulp.

We finally got hold of him. We hung on until he calmed down. He kept trying to shake loose and go after Neal or Denny—he didn't care which.

"Neal put him up to it," José kept snarling. "Denny's too dumb to think of that himself. Neal put him up to it. He was gonna rip you up with those things, Pat. It's cheating! It's not fair!"

José was probably right. Still, I wasn't hurt and there wasn't any sense starting a big fight over it.

"I wasn't trying to hurt him," Denny lied. "I've worn them before. Nobody ever said anything." That was a lie too.

Then Neal jumped in.

"There ain't no rules about wearing cleats."

Now I knew it was a setup.

"Guys in high school wear them all the time," Neal insisted.

"Yeah," somebody yelled from the back of the gang. "They wear football cleats. *Not* track cleats."

It would have probably blown up into a big fight if Larry Palmer hadn't stepped in.

He motioned Charlie Ratcliff aside for a conference. It took only a second for them to talk it over and return to the group.

"It's our decision," Larry said, clearing his throat, "that no matter what Denny says, Neal probably put him up to wearing the cleats."

"They're not even his shoes," Charlie jumped in. "Look how big they are. They're probably his older brother's."

Larry cleared his throat again.

"Anyway," he announced, "it's our decision that if Pat gets stitches from being ripped up by cleats, it doesn't count. Furthermore, Denny doesn't get to play football with us for two weeks."

Neal took his football and went inside. Most of his team followed him. The game was over.

The next football game, Jimmy got to come back. His mother made him wear a football helmet, though, because of his banging his head on the pecan tree. He should have been watching where he was going instead of trying to sneak a peek at Tiffany Williams. So having to wear a helmet probably served him right. None of the other guys wore helmets, but we figured it was all right for Jimmy.

The next day Doug Loy showed up with his helmet, too. He said his mother told him to wear it because of what had happened to Jimmy. So we let him.

Then, about halfway through the game, it happened. I dropped back. All my receivers were running downfield. Larry was running out, trying to get away from B.B., so he could catch the ball. Charlie was covering Curt, but Curt had a step or two on him. All my other receivers were covered. Since Curt had a step or two on Charlie, and since he was so tall, I drew back and passed to him.

I overthrew him a bit, figuring he had the best chance of jumping and completing the pass. Charlie raced after Curt. Curt jumped for the ball. Everybody watched.

At that very instant—timed down to the second—Neal and Doug both rushed me.

I guess I should have known something like that would happen. I didn't expect them to tackle me *after* the pass was off. That was roughing the passer.

Suddenly Neal had me by the shoulders. Only, instead of trying to throw me to the ground like he usually did, he was holding me up. Real straight.

And just as he had me standing up—stretched out—Doug came flying in. He lowered his head.

I saw the sunlight reflecting off the top of his shiny helmet. I tried to double over and protect myself with my shoulder. Neal held me tight.

Doug ran headfirst into my side. His rock-hard football helmet cracked against my ribs. Stars flashed. The pain raced across my chest. The air whooshed out of me. Clutching my side, I fell.

CHAPTER
11

I was sitting on the ground, still clutching my side, when I woke up. My whole chest was throbbing and pounding. A couple of the guys had their shirts off and were fanning me with them. José and Kent knelt beside me. Kent was slapping my cheek, real gentle, with his hand. José's nose was almost touching mine. He looked straight into my eyes.

"You okay, Pat? You awake? You alive?"

I still couldn't get my breath, so I grunted at him and nodded. Neal had snuck to the back of the crowd. I could see him smiling.

Then I held tighter to the throbbing pain in my side. It hurt so bad, I wanted to cry.

I guess I had already been crying. My cheeks felt wet. I didn't want the other guys to see, so I kind of ducked my head and tried to rub my cheeks on my shoulder.

"What happened?" I heard Charlie ask. He was someplace behind the guys who were fanning me with their shirts, and I couldn't see him.

"Doug tackled him right as he was throwing the ball," Neal answered. "I was watching the whole thing. It was a good, clean tackle."

I shook my head. I still couldn't talk.

"Is that what happened?" Larry asked from someplace behind me.

I shook my head again.

"Neal held me," I gasped. "Doug . . ." Puff, puff. "Hit me . . . " Pant, puff. "With helmet . . . while Neal held me . . . up."

"That's a lie," Neal squealed, shoving his way through the crowd of guys. "I never touched him. I never got near him."

I shook my head again. Still doubled over, I held my chest with one hand and pointed with the other to my shoulders.

"Held me . . . stood me up so . . . Doug could hit me . . . helmet . . . hard!"

"Did not!" Doug called from beside me. "I hit him with my shoulder. I never touched him with my helmet. Besides, I didn't even tackle him that hard."

"Yeah," Neal added. "I bet he hurt himself when he fell. You know what a klutz he is."

José was still looking me straight in the eye. I guess he was trying to see if I could focus on him or if I was still kind of out of it. Suddenly his big, burly black eyebrow dipped. He spun around and jumped to his feet.

"You're a liar, Doug Loy! You and Neal both! You're nothin' but sneakin' liars!"

He started after them, only the guys stopped him. Larry asked if he'd seen what happened. José shook his head. Then Larry asked Kent.

"No, I was watchin' Curt jump for that pass, like everybody else," he answered honestly. "But I do know you don't get hurt that bad from a regular tackle. I know they did somethin' to Pat."

Neal shoved one of the guys who was fanning me with his shirt. I glanced up and saw Neal glaring down at me.

"Pat's the liar! He fell down and hurt himself, like he always does. I bet his ribs are broke or something, and he's scared his mommy will make him go to the doctor. He just don't want to pay off the bet. He figures if he whines and cries about it enough, tries to make out like it's *our* fault, he won't have to kiss The Blimp." He jabbed a finger at me. "Pat's the liar. He's the sneak. We didn't do nothin' to him!"

I was amazed at Neal's little speech. He was so convincing and sincere that, for a second, I found *myself* trying to remember what happened. Then the throbbing in my side gouged me again. No matter how believable Neal acted, *I remembered what happened.*

Larry and Charlie tried to find out if any of the other guys had seen it. Like Kent, they had all been watching the ball, to see if Curt was going to catch it. Finally the two judges went over to Neal's porch for another conference.

I sat clutching my side and rocking back and forth on the ground. Neal stood above me, glaring down with a smug little smirk on his face. Kent and Herb Scott hung on to José.

Last time the judges had a conference, it took them about two seconds. This time they must have talked things over for a good twenty minutes. By the time they got up and started toward us, I could breathe again. The guys had helped me to my feet.

"Nobody really saw what happened," Larry announced. "Neal says he didn't touch Pat. Doug says he made a good clean tackle. And Pat says Neal held

him up so Doug could dive into him with his helmet . . ."

All three of us nodded.

". . . but nobody saw it."

I frowned, nodding my agreement. Doug and
Neal nodded too. Only they were smiling.

"So . . ." he continued, "since nobody saw it, and
two guys say one thing and Pat says something else,
we've decided that . . ." He hesitated, again, like
he really didn't want to say what he was going to.
Charlie kind of nudged him with an elbow. Larry
shrugged. "It's our decision that the tackle counts.
If Pat's got a busted rib—it counts."

His eyes were sort of sad as he looked at me. Neal
clapped his hands together.

"He's got to go to the doctor, right?"

Charlie and Larry nodded.

"And if he's got so much as one broken rib, he has
to kiss The Blimp."

They nodded again.

Neal popped Doug on the shoulder with his hand.
It was all he could do to keep from laughing. "All
right, dude. Way to go."

Then he caught himself. He glanced back at me
and tried to act concerned.

"Hope you're not hurt too bad, Pat."

Still half doubled over, I just looked at him.

Larry's eyes narrowed when he tugged at Neal's sleeve.

"We've also decided somethin' else. From now on, if Pat gets hurt playing football, baseball, or basketball . . ."

"Any kind of contact sport," Charlie explained.

"Yeah," Larry went on. "If he gets hurt playing any kind of sport where Neal, Doug, or B.B. are on the field—it *don't count!*"

Neal's mouth kind of fell open.

"What are we gonna do the rest of the summer if we can't play football?" he yelped.

Charlie shrugged. "We can still play football. It just doesn't count if Pat gets hurt."

Neal stuck his nose in the air. He looked around for his football, snatched it off the ground, and stormed off for his house.

Last time he took his ball and went home, most of his team followed him. This time only about four guys trailed Neal to his front door. On the top step to his porch, he turned and glared at me.

"Just like you, Berry," he snarled. "We've been having some great football games. Then you go and hurt yourself and mess up the whole summer.

"*Fat Pat Berry, the Twinkletoes Fairy—The Klutz* . . . If you ain't tough enough to take a little ol' tackle, you shouldn't even be on the field." He turned and went inside. He slammed the door and muttered, loud enough for all of us to hear, "Sissy. Big fat klutz."

As the guys helped me down the street to the law office where Mama worked, I realized that the Fat Pat Berry stuff hurt even more than my ribs.

CHAPTER

12

I think we scared Mama half to death.

She must have seen us coming up the street, because she came flying through the front door of her office before José could even open it.

I don't think it scared her that I was walking kind of bent over to one side. I don't think it scared her that José and Kent were kind of carrying me, one under each arm, like soldiers helping a wounded comrade off a battlefield. I think what scared her was that it took a whole herd of guys to bring me downtown. There were about nine boys behind us, each looking worried and concerned as we made our way down Main Street.

Without giving José or Kent a chance to tell her what happened, she dug in her purse for her keys. She stuck the keys in her mouth and stuffed her

purse under her arm. Then she moved Kent and
José aside, and we headed for the car.

Mama's driving, as we raced across town to the
hospital, scared me even more than thinking my
ribs might be broken. I felt like we were at the Indy
500. We dodged in and out of traffic, zipped through
yellow lights, and screeched around corners. If I
had had a choice, I'd rather have kissed The Blimp
than been killed in a car wreck.

"I'm all right," I said, trying to calm Mama down.
"My side really doesn't hurt anymore."

My ploy didn't work.

We waited forever in one of the little emergency
rooms. A woman in a white uniform asked Mama all
sorts of questions. None of them seemed to have
anything to do with my being hurt. Then a doctor
came in. He was a tall, skinny young man with gold-
rimmed glasses that sat right on the tip of his nose.
He asked me to tell him all about what happened. It
was hard to do, since he stuck a thermometer in my
mouth and I could hardly talk. He also punched
around on my ribs, which made it hard to talk, too.

When I kept jumping, he turned to Mama.

"Better take a few X rays. Might have a broken
rib or two.

*   *   *

I sat in a cold chair in the cold X-ray room. There were all sorts of machines around. A nurse came in and told me to take my shirt off. I got even colder. The nurse turned some switches and rattled around in a little room with a window in it. While she was getting everything ready, I had time to think.

So what if I had a cracked rib? It wasn't any worse than the broken leg or my broken arm. I'd survive.

"Stand up here," she said, motioning me to this thing on the wall. "Put your chin on top and lean your shoulders forward."

The metal that cradled my chin felt hard and cold as she raised it up so high that it stretched my neck.

So what if I had to kiss The Blimp? I frowned and kind of wiggled.

"Stand still, please."

"Yes, ma'am."

She went to the little room with the window. "Real still."

I grunted.

Why did I keep calling Kristine Plimpton "The Blimp"? Melony Parks was twice as fat as Kristine. Nobody called her a blimp. Kristine was just a little plump.

Neal was the one who got everybody to call her

The Blimp. That's what made me decide I didn't like playing with her anymore. That's when I stopped talking to her.

I smiled.

One time she came over with her parents, and she stuffed ice down my back. It was kind of funny, the way I squealed and jumped around. I chased her all over the house, trying to get even with her. We laughed and giggled till I thought I was going to pee in my pants.

Even when our folks made us quit, Kristine still laughed at me. Only she laughed with those brown eyes. Those brown eyes that sparkled and seemed to cut right through me.

"Take a deep breath and hold it."

I jerked, suddenly realizing where I was. I took a deep breath and tried not to move.

So what? I could survive kissing Kristine Plimpton in front of the whole school. It wouldn't be great . . . but I would survive it. Just like I survived the broken arm and the broken leg and the five stitches where Dad hit me with the door. I was gonna be all right.

*   *   *

"Come on, kid. Be still! Take another deep breath and hold it."

I'd had X rays before, but the X-ray room was still scary. It was cold. The metal pushed my chin up, and my side throbbed from the deep breath. And . . . with my eyes closed . . .

Kristine stood there. The whole school watched as she puckered up. I could hardly see her pretty brown eyes over those pudgy cheeks of hers. Then those fat lips came closer and closer and closer and . . .

Even with my eyes closed, the room began to spin. My head felt light. My stomach rolled. I felt weak. Everything went black.

The guys were waiting in my driveway. Mama got out and came around the car to help me.

José ran up beside us. He looked worried.

"Is he all right, Mrs. Berry?"

Mama smiled and ruffled José's hair.

"He's fine. Doctor said his ribs were just bruised and he'd have to take it easy for a day or two. But he's okay."

"What's the Band-Aid on his forehead for?" José's question was almost a gasp.

Mama shrugged.

"He fainted while they were taking the X rays and bumped his head when he fell."

José shuddered. "Stitches?"

Mama shook her head. "No. Just a scratch. He's fine."

José heaved a sigh of relief. So did the herd of guys behind him.

I could have died when Mama told them that I fainted. Guys don't faint! I mean . . . it was bad enough being called a fat twinkletoes fairy or The Klutz. Now the others could start laughing about what a wimp or a sissy I was. And if the guys ever found out that just the thought of kissing The Blimp was the reason . . .

I could walk just fine, so I wouldn't let Mama help me to the front door. The pack of guys followed. At the steps Mama turned to them.

"I'm keeping him inside the rest of today," she announced. "And the rest of the weekend, too. He needs to rest for a couple of days." She kind of waved her purse at them. "You guys go on and play."

Mama made me stay in bed all day. She called her office and said she wouldn't be back until Monday.

While I was lying in my room waiting for supper, I got to thinking again.

I hated being known as Fat Pat Berry, the Twinkletoes Fairy. I hated being The Klutz. I could just hear the guys talking about me while they walked home. "Fat Pat Berry, the Twinkletoes Fairy . . . yeah, The Klutz. He faints, too. What a wimp."

It made me want to puke.

There wasn't anything I could do about fainting. I couldn't help being a klutz, either. But maybe I *could* do something about the fat stuff and the twinkletoes bit.

Even if José and Kent wouldn't stay around to take care of me after school started, I was somehow going to get rid of the Fat part of my name. I'd stay away from peanut butter on celery. And cookies to help the taste of carrots. And candy bars from the refrigerator. *No more!*

Mama fixed corn on the cob, macaroni and cheese, and steaks for supper.

I ate the steak. I ate the corn, only I didn't put any butter on it. And instead of the macaroni and cheese, I ate some carrots.

There was ice cream for dessert. I kind of played with it instead of eating it. When we were about finished, I looked at Mama and Dad.

"I don't want to take dance lessons next year, okay?"

"Why?" Dad had his elbow on the table. He propped his chin in his palm and looked at me.

I shrugged. "I don't know. It's just not fun anymore."

His tongue moved around the inside of his mouth and made a bulge in the side of his cheek. "Is it because it's not fun, or because you're afraid some of the guys are going to make fun of you?"

"Ah . . . well . . . not, ah . . ." I stammered, unable to tell him about the pestering Neal had done all year.

"If it's something *you* really want," Dad said, tilting his head to one side, "that's one thing. If you want out of dance because you're trying to gain your friends' approval . . ." He shook his head. "That's not the way to do it. You have to learn to make *your* decisions, not let someone else make them for you."

I tinked my spoon against the side of my ice-cream bowl. I chewed at my bottom lip.

Dad reached across the table and punched me on the shoulder. It wasn't hard, just kind of a shove.

"Let's talk about it again later," he said softly.

CHAPTER

13

"So what did they say?" José asked me that Monday morning on our way to Doug Loy's house. Saturday had been Doug's birthday. His dad had gotten him a new basketball goal. They put it up at the edge of the driveway, not too far from the chain-link fence and Tiffany Williams's pool.

"They said they'd think about it." I sighed. "Mama said that she had already talked to Mr. Paramore. He told her that guys my age usually wanted to quit because of what he called peer pressure. That means they want to quit because the other guys start making fun of them. He said that I was getting pretty good, and if I'd just stick with it awhile longer . . ."

"What about your dad?"

"He said we'd talk about it later."

"Just tell them how much you hate dance lessons. Tell 'em you're gonna kill yourself if they don't let you quit."

I shrugged.

"But I don't hate them. They're kind of fun in a way. Besides, I'm getting pretty good at the tap and jazz parts."

José shrugged.

"Well, tell 'em, anyway. You don't like being called a twinkletoes fairy, do you?"

I shook my head. "Why don't you quit band?" I asked. "You don't like being called a wimp, do you?"

He didn't answer. We shuffled along a ways without saying much. Kent met us at the corner. Tina and Katrina Bertwilder were playing with their roller skates. The Bertwilders lived in the corner house, three doors down from me. The twins, Tina and Katrina, were about five or so. Tina was kind of wobbly when she stood up. She asked Kent to give her a shove. Gently he gave her a little push.

"Me too," Katrina called. Kent pretended he didn't hear her and trotted over to join us.

"I'm glad you're okay, Pat," he greeted me. "I'm glad they didn't bust your ribs."

I smiled.

"This is getting crazy," he said as we walked. "I

mean, making a bet is one thing. This bet could get you killed, Pat. They really tried to hurt you."

I nodded and smiled again.

"I think we should call the bet off," Kent said. "I think we ought to tell Neal to forget the whole thing. You could get hurt. What do you think, José?"

José stopped walking. Kent and I stopped, too.

"I don't know." He shrugged. "I don't want Pat to get hurt. I mean . . ." He smiled at me. His eyebrow sort of waved at one end. "Pat's a good friend. You don't like to see your friends get hurt. Still . . ."

Kent nodded. "I don't want Pat to get hurt, either. But I guess I don't think we should call off the bet. I'm tired of being called Kent Green, the String Bean. I'd love to see Neal Moffett stand on the steps the first day of school and plant a big, sloppy kiss on The Blimp."

All three of us laughed. Then the sound of someone crying came from behind us. We glanced back. Tina had fallen and landed flat on her bottom. We quit laughing, afraid she might think we were laughing at her. After a moment her twin sister helped her up.

"Bet he won't do it," José said as we rounded the corner at the end of Doug's block. "I bet if he loses, he'll chicken out. Bet he won't kiss her."

This time Kent stopped. His skinny shoulders seemed to widen.

"No way, dude. Neal can't chicken out. If he does, the whole school will know what a coward he is."

A bunch of the guys were already playing basketball when we got to Doug's house. Doug's mother thought basketball in the driveway was a lot safer than football with the pecan trees. Neal and Bobby weren't around. I was glad.

Still, fourteen was too many for a basketball game, so we chose up three teams. Two teams played to twenty-one while the other kept a vigil on Tiffany Williams's backyard. When the game was over, the winners had to play the team on the sideline and the other team watched for Tiffany.

My team was resting when she finally came out. We signaled the others. The game slowed down as Tiffany climbed onto the air mattress. It slowed down again when she reached back and unsnapped her top.

Charlie's team beat Kent's team. We went out on the court and were just about to start the second game when Denny Perrin got the ball.

"I got an idea," he whispered, motioning us to follow him to the edge of the driveway.

Butch and Ben met us when we neared the chain-link fence. Their pug noses wrinkled up and their little fluff tails flopped over their backs as they yapped and barked at us.

Tiffany raised her head from the mattress. We all turned around and acted like we were looking in the other direction and talking about something important. After a while Denny peeked over his shoulder.

"Okay," he whispered.

We turned around. Tiffany was facing the other direction. Denny drew back the basketball and chunked it toward the pool.

Our hopes soared as it flew through the air. Our eyes grew wide when it hit the water, not two feet from that yellow bikini. We gasped as the cold water splashed across Tiffany's bare, dry back.

She jerked, but she didn't rise up.

Our hearts went plop on the ground when all she did was lift her head and look at us.

"How do girls do that?" Curt Johnson sounded totally disgusted. "I mean, if somebody splashed cold water on me, I'd come up swinging. I'd at least jump off my air mattress. How do girls do that?"

"Whoops," Denny called. "I dropped the basketball. I'll come and get it."

Butch and Ben snarled and yapped louder as he took hold of the fence. They spun in circles, showing their tiny, snippy little white teeth. They wanted that leg to come over the fence. They wanted to chew it clear off.

"Don't bother," Tiffany called back. "I'll get it for you."

With that, she reached back and fastened the strap to her bikini. Slick as a greased pig sliding under a fence, she just snapped it. Then she sat up and paddled her mattress over to get the ball.

"How do they do that?" Curt wondered again.

She threw the ball to us. Disappointed, we went back to our game.

Bobby and Neal showed up on their skateboards about thirty minutes later. They came wheeling into Doug's driveway. Neal jumped off his board, popped the back end with his foot, and caught it.

"Come on, you guys. Go get your skateboards and let's go cruise around some."

Everybody stopped playing.

"I don't have a skateboard," Ben Steward said.

"Me neither," Herb Scott added.

"I don't either," somebody else said.

"Where we going?" Doug's voice sounded excited.

"Downtown," Bobby answered. "We can run the

parking garage on Fifth Street. The ramp's kind of steep, but it's safe."

Somehow the words sounded like he had been rehearsing what he was going to say. I can't really explain it. It was just too clear and neat for Bobby. He didn't even sniff or wipe his nose on his shirt.

Everyone except Doug Loy and Gary Pitts shook his head and started back to play basketball.

"Come on, you guys," Neal almost pleaded. "It'll be fun."

"Nah," Pepper Young said. "Most of us don't even have skateboards."

"I got a skateboard," Larry said. "My mom won't let me take it downtown, though. Too many cars."

Neal walked up to me. "Come on, Pat. You got a skateboard. You'll go with us, won't you?"

Kent was standing on the free-throw line. He was about to make a foul shot, because Denny Perrin had slapped his arm while he'd been shooting. He aimed at the basket. Then he stopped and tucked the ball under his arm.

"Sounds to me like you and B.B. figured a way of getting Pat hurt," he said. "What you gonna do, shove him out in front of a car or something?"

Neal tried to look innocent.

"You can come with us, String Bean. You got a

skateboard, too. You can come and watch. We won't even touch the little baby."

His lip really curled when he looked back at me.

"Come on, Pat. What's wrong—*chicken?*" Then, louder, so Tiffany as well as the rest of the guys could hear. "Not only are you *fat*. Now you're *chicken*, too. Fat Pat Berry, the *chicken* Twinkletoes Fairy." He put his hands on his hips and shook his head. "You're such a *chicken klutz*, you'd probably break your arm just trying to get on a skateboard."

I didn't have a chance to open my mouth and say something back to him before José was there. Instead of trying to hit Neal, like I first figured he was gonna do, José reached into his hip pocket and slipped out a sheet of paper. He unfolded it and stuck it right in Neal's face.

"Says right here, Neal. Pat doesn't have to do anything unless *all of us do it*." He stabbed at Rule Seven with his finger and kept stuffing the sheet closer to Neal's nose. With a jerk of his head, he motioned at Bobby.

"Why don't you and your snot-nosed little friend just bug off. Go . . . go to . . ." He kind of cleared his throat. "Go play in the traffic or something."

Then he turned and went back to the basketball game.

Neal was in a regular snit. He slammed his skateboard down so hard, I thought the wheels would pop off. Bobby tugged at his arm and they left.

The next two times we got together to play basketball, we didn't see either one of them. Pepper said he'd seen them in Neal's backyard. He said they had hammers and saws and it looked like they were building something, only he didn't stop to find out what.

Without Neal around trying to be the leader and boss everybody, we had fun playing. We also had fun trying to figure out new plans to get Tiffany to lift up off her air mattress. None of us could figure out anything that worked. I guess we were all thinking the same thing as Curt Johnson:

"How can girls do that?"

Three weeks before school started, Neal and Bobby joined our group again. This time, they had something that *all of us* could do.

I guess getting close to the deadline made them sort of creative. I guess it made Neal a little desperate, too.

None of us dreamed how creative or how desperate Neal Moffett could get.

CHAPTER

14

Bobby Blaton and Neal Moffett had built a bicycle course. It was a creation of true beauty. We went over to see it and, for a time, forgot all about the yellow bikini.

"Everybody has a bike," Neal said as he showed us through the course. He turned to José. "Remember the boards we put on those blocks at your house last summer? Remember how much fun we had jumping our bikes on the ramp you built?"

José nodded.

"Well this thing is even more fun," Neal boasted. "We got four jumping ramps. Got cones to weave in and out of. Even got a balance-beam thing you have to cross. This is the greatest bicycle course ever built. Look!" He held up a leather strap. A shiny watch dangled from the end. "My dad got me a new stopwatch for my birthday. We can even time each other."

"I'm first!" Rick Davis yelled, rolling his bike to the back of Neal's house, where the course started.

"Me next," Pepper said as he raced after him.

"I'll get my bicycle." Doug trotted off.

Most of the guys had their bikes with them. Kent, José, and I all lived so close to Doug's and Neal's that we didn't need our bikes.

Neal cocked an eyebrow and smiled at José and me.

"You guys gonna go get your bikes, too? Or are you gonna chicken out?"

José put his hands on his hips. "What happened to the dirt bike your dad was gonna get you?"

Neal looked at his watch. "He changed his mind. Said he'd get it for me next year." Then, looking at me instead of José, he said, "So you gonna get your bikes, or be a bunch of chickens?"

José's eyebrow started wiggling as he looked at the course. It went up and down so fast, it looked like a wave on the ocean. Finally he sighed. "Come on, Pat, let's go get our bikes."

"That balance-beam thing is dangerous," Kent said. "It's set real close to that one jump ramp. If your front tire slips off the thing, you could crack your head on the other ramp."

"Did you see all those nails sticking out?" José asked me.

I shrugged. "Yeah, but with B.B. and Neal, it's hard to tell whether they left them on purpose or whether they're just sloppy at building stuff."

"On purpose!" José snorted. "Neal's figuring on getting you hurt. There's a bunch of things you could get hurt on—like that big ramp. You know, the last jump, where you end up landing in the road?"

"I think it's stupid," Kent pouted.

At the sidewalk to my house, José stopped. There was almost a twinkle in his dark eyes.

"Kent, you and Pat get your bikes. I'll go get mine and meet you here on the sidewalk. I got an idea."

When Kent, José, and I rode our bikes into Neal Moffett's backyard an hour later, Neal's eyes almost fell clear out of his head. Some of the guys laughed. Then Neal's mouth dropped open. It gaped so wide, I thought his bottom lip would get stuck in his zipper.

The other guys, who were waiting their turn to

ride the course, dropped their bikes and trotted over to take a closer look at the strange sight in Neal Moffett's backyard. Even Ben Steward, who was cautiously riding his bicycle across the long two-by-six board Neal had set up as a balance beam, stopped. He jumped off his bike and pushed it over to where I was standing.

"It's a Martian!" Herb Scott chuckled.

"No," Gary Pitts laughed. "It's one of King Arthur's knights—straight from the Round Table."

"I don't know *what it is!*" Rick Davis said. He stood in front of me and tilted his head so far to one side, I thought he might tip over. "I've never seen anything like it!"

Everybody laughed again, then started circling around me. I laughed too. I couldn't help it.

A medieval knight or some alien from outer space sounded like a pretty good description to me. It had taken José and Kent so long to get me dressed, I hadn't had time to check myself out in a mirror. Still, I could imagine how I looked.

José had made me put on his old catcher's mask from Little League. He had also called Kent and asked him to ride his bicycle out to the high school to visit with his dad. Kent's dad had a set of keys to the locker room. José wanted Kent to find the smallest set of shoulder pads and football pants that he could.

When Kent called from the high school, José answered the phone. I pulled off the catcher's mask so I could listen in on the extension phone in the kitchen.

"My dad says there's an old uniform that they don't use anymore," Kent had told us. "We have to bring it back before school starts though."

"Does it have shoulder pads and a helmet with it?" José wondered.

"Yeah."

"What's the deal with the mask and shoulder pads?" I interrupted.

"Rule Eight says if everybody plays, you have to play, too, Pat," José answered. "But there's nothing in the rules about wearing protective clothes. Now hurry up with that stuff, Kent."

When Kent arrived, I tried on the helmet, but it was too small, so while Kent rode back to the high school to get another one, José dragged me to his front yard.

Outside, beside José's bicycle, was a long, cardboard carpet tube. José's family had put new carpet in their den during the summer. The carpet had arrived wrapped around the tube. José got me to help him drag the tube over to Dad's workroom.

José measured the space from my armpit to my elbow. Then he got one of Dad's handsaws and cut off a chunk of cardboard tubing. He measured the distance from my elbow to my wrist. Then he measured my ankle to my knee and cut some more cardboard.

We had played with carpet tubing before. Last summer I stuck my whole arm into the end of the tube that the new carpet for our living room was wrapped around. But now, when José tried to shove my arm into the first chunk he'd cut up, it wouldn't go through. He squeezed my arm and frowned.

"Been lifting too many weights." He grinned.

He took the saw and split the tube lengthwise. He shoved my arm through it and taped the part he'd cut with that gray duct-tape stuff. The second piece, from my wrist to my elbow, slid on just fine. He split the tube for the other arm. When he tried to fit my legs through the tubes that went from my knees to my ankles he had to split them, as well. Guess my legs had developed muscles, too.

"Have to count on the football pants to protect your upper leg," he said. "There's no way we're gonna get this tubing over those humongous thighs of yours."

When Kent got back from the high-school locker

room, José put the catcher's mask over my face. Kent had brought a huge helmet. It fit over the mask *and* my head. José tightened the chin strap.

Then we had to take the helmet and mask off so we could get the shoulder pads on me. When those were strapped in place, we got the mask and helmet back on.

After I was all dressed, I had a catcher's mask over my face, a football helmet on my head, and shoulder pads over my shoulders. I was wearing football pants, with pads to protect my thighs. I was covered with cardboard tubing from my wrists to my armpits and from my ankles to my knees. (José left a gap at my elbow and knees so I could bend. Otherwise I couldn't have walked, much less ridden my bike.)

Finally José had taped Dad's thick welding gloves on my hands and attached them to the cardboard just above my wrist.

I could barely move. I felt like the Tin Man in *The Wizard of Oz*. I probably looked as funny as I felt.

Neal was the only one who didn't laugh. He sat pouting by the water faucet near the beginning of the course.

"It ain't fair! He can't wear all that stuff. It ain't fair."

José trotted over to him. He reached into his hip pocket and pulled out the crumpled sheet of rules. He held it out for Neal to read.

"Show me where it says Pat can't wear protective clothing."

Neal glanced at the sheet. He glared up at José.

"It ain't fair!"

José cocked his black eyebrow.

"Come on," Kent called. "I'll ride next. You time me, Neal."

Neal crushed the leather strap of his stopwatch in his hand. He jabbed the little button like it was an ant he was trying to squash on the sidewalk.

José rode after Kent. Then it was my turn. How I made it, I still don't know. It took me twice as long as it did Kent and José to inch my way through the bicycle course. I could hardly bend my neck enough to see where my front tires were—but I made it. José stood at the jump that ended on Twentieth Street just to make *extra* sure there weren't any cars coming when I finished the course.

A couple of the other guys went next, then Kent, José, and me again.

This time I missed the balance beam. A two-by-six piece of wood is huge when you lug it around to help your dad build something. But when you're trying to ride a bicycle over it, it looks tiny. I missed it with my front tire.

I landed on my shoulder pads and helmet. I wasn't hurt. Only, when I tried to get up, I couldn't.

I rolled to my other side and tried to get my elbows under me. That didn't work either. So I decided to roll over onto my stomach.

I felt, and probably looked, like a total idiot. I was rolling from side to side, flopping around. My arms and legs, stiff because of the cardboard, flailed in all directions as I tried to get off my back.

"Look." Larry Palmer laughed. "It's a Ninja Turtle. He's stuck on his back and can't get up. Let's go help him."

All the guys clumped around me. Only instead of helping me up, they just laughed. I got to giggling, too. I kept flopping and flouncing around. I really put on a show for them. At last they got me on my feet and propped me up.

We laughed so hard, we couldn't catch our breath. Finally I told them to quit. "If you get me too tickled," I said, "I'm gonna have to go to the bathroom. It's gonna take thirty minutes to get this stuff off so I can reach my zipper."

José came up and whomped me on the shoulder pads.

"You're my best friend, Pat," he announced, "but you better quit laughing, 'cause I'm sure not gonna unzip your pants and help you go to the bathroom. I don't care how good a friend you are."

That really got everybody started. I laughed so hard, I fell down again, and the guys had to help me back on my feet.

Finally, when we straightened up a little, Charlie Ratcliff got his bike. "My turn on the course," he called. "Ready to time me, Neal?"

Neal sat against the water faucet. He glared at all of us. Then he jumped to his feet. He squeezed his stopwatch so hard, his knuckles turned white.

"This bicycle course is dumb. It's stupid." He threw the new stopwatch on the ground. "Somebody else time it. I'm going inside to watch TV."

Nobody laughed. Nobody left, either.

Bobby trotted over and picked up the watch. His eyes seemed to sparkle like little round BBs as he looked at it. He wiped his nose on his arm and turned to Charlie.

"I'll time you. Go!"

CHAPTER

15

We'd had so much fun riding the bicycle course and laughing over my armor, it was a real disappointment when we went back the next day and found Neal's backyard empty. He'd torn down the ramps and stacked the wood against his house.

Neal and Bobby were nowhere around and no one answered the door, so we went to Doug's house for basketball and bikinis.

It took the guys about ten minutes to strip my protective gear off so I could play. We had a couple of pretty good games.

Tiffany came out. She had on her hot-pink bikini.

I was beginning to think that Tiffany and the air mattress had passed the point of being simply interesting. I mean, sure, we were curious—most guys are. But this had become more than just curiosity. Now it was a challenge. It was a boy-girl thing, kind of like the girls beating us at kickball in second grade or beating us at math races in fifth grade. Tiffany was determined *not* to rise up off her mattress. That made us even *more* determined to find a way to get her to.

As usual she was one step ahead of us.

Girls are like that, I guess.

I don't think even a stick of dynamite would have lifted Tiffany off that air mattress. It didn't keep us from trying, though.

She lay on her back for a while. Then, when she rolled over and unsnapped her top, Pepper Young motioned us over to the fence. Butch and Ben were still in the house, so our approach was totally silent. There was nothing to tip off Tiffany that we were moving closer. Her eyes were closed. Even though her head was on the mattress facing us, she never so much as fluttered an eyelash.

Pepper was the only guy in school who was considered fatter than me. Nobody ever called him fatso or lard-butt, though. Along with being fat, he was big. He was a whole head taller than most of us, and nobody messed with him. We figured that if we did, he'd sit on us and smother us to death. Along with being big, he was pretty sharp, too.

We could hardly wait to see what idea he had come up with to get Tiffany to remove her bikini top.

At the fence he cupped his hands to his mouth.

"Look!" he screamed. "Up there! It's the Good-year blimp."

About half the guys looked up. The rest of us—knowing the Goodyear blimp would never in a million years come flying over our neighborhood—kept our eyes glued to that loose hot-pink bikini top.

Our hearts pounded in our ears. Our breath came in short gasps.

Tiffany opened one eye and glanced up. That was all. Then she looked at us, smiled, and closed her eyes again.

"How do they do that?" Curt wondered.

The next day the backboard fell off Doug's basketball goal. It almost squashed Herb Scott and Ben Steward, but they managed to jump aside before it crashed to the driveway.

When we inspected it and found nothing was broken, the only thing we could figure was someone had loosened the bolts. All eyes turned to Doug.

"I didn't do it!" Doug yelped. With his finger he

made an X across his chest. "I swear. I didn't even know it was loose."

Denny Perrin glared at him. "You haven't made one lay-up all morning. Pat's quick getting to the inside. He usually shoots a lot of lay-ups. But not you." He growled. "Every shot you've taken has been from outside."

"Yeah," others muttered. "Doug never did go for the basket."

Pepper Young towered above Doug. "You might not have done it," he said, "but if Neal or B.B. undid the bolts, I bet you knew about it."

"No . . . I didn't see a thing . . . I . . ." Doug stammered. "Honest . . . I swear. They came over, but B.B. and I were looking at magazines. Neal went outside, but I didn't know . . ."

Pepper stuck his hands on his hips. His nostrils flared as he looked down his nose at Doug.

Doug swore that he didn't have anything to do with it. Finally he went inside and got some of his dad's tools. With a ladder from the garage and the tools, we fixed the backboard and returned to our game.

Neal and Bobby didn't show up the following day, either. We played basketball, and when Tiffany came out, we sat down to eat. Rick Davis ate fast.

He drank his Coke almost in one gulp. Then, with a sneaky smile, he drank the rest of Larry's pop and asked if he could have half of my Diet Dr. Pepper.

After he finished, Rick kind of leaned against the pecan tree and rubbed his stomach. When Tiffany Williams unsnapped the top to her bikini, Rick struggled to his feet and motioned us to the fence. When he sucked in a deep breath and started making that clicking sound down deep in his throat, we all knew what was coming.

Rick Davis could burp. I don't mean burp—I mean *burp*!

It was a talent that most of us had mastered by third or fourth grade. Rick, however, was the leading expert in the entire school. He kept sucking in air and making that clicking sound. Then he cupped his hands to his mouth.

Anticipation made my teeth grind together. Most of us clamped our hands over our mouths and noses to keep from laughing. Rick took one last breath. His eyes kind of crossed.

Then Rick Davis let it rip!

It's a shame that somebody from the *Guinness Book of World Records* wasn't there. I think if they had been, Rick's burp would have made the book.

The belch that came out of him was one of those low, rolling, rumbling sounds. It was so deep, it didn't come from the pit of his stomach. It came clear up from the tips of his toes. Though no one timed it, it must have lasted well over a minute. The volume never decreased, either. The end of the burp was still as loud as the beginning. It was so loud and gross, we stuck our fingers in our ears. The leaves on Doug Loy's pecan tree seemed to shake. Even Butch and Ben perked up their droopy ears. Their little fluff Pomeranian tails stuck straight in the air as they looked around, trying to find the strange creature that could make such a sound.

When the last puff of air rumbled from Rick and he almost collapsed on the ground, we all clapped. In amazement we had been watching him instead of Tiffany. Suddenly remembering, we turned to look.

Tiffany hadn't moved a muscle. She still lay flat on her stomach. The only movement was the little ripples that scampered across the surface of the pool, forming circles around her air mattress. There was no sound of laughter, just the ripples.

I guess even girls can appreciate such an exceptional talent.

Tiffany rolled her head to the side and looked. She tried to hide her smile, but she couldn't. Never losing contact with the air mattress, she fastened her top and went inside.

"How do they do that?" Curt chuckled.

The other guys patted Rick on the back. I shook his hand. After congratulating him on his record-setting burp, we went back to our basketball game and tried to figure out something new to get Tiffany's attention for tomorrow.

Just as we were leaving, Doug motioned Larry Palmer to the side. Frowning, I knew something was going on. I could tell by the way Doug's eyes darted around and by the way he leaned close to Larry's ear when he whispered something to him. It made me nervous. I knew something was up, only I didn't know what.

CHAPTER

16

I didn't worry about it long. Right before supper Larry Palmer called me.

"Doug Loy told me somethin' this afternoon." Larry cleared his throat. "But you got to promise not to tell. Okay?"

"Okay."

"I mean, you got to swear. If Neal ever finds out that Doug squealed . . . well . . . you got to swear."

"Okay, Larry. I swear."

He sighed. "Tomorrow Neal and B.B. are gonna show up at the basketball game. They been working on a bicycle ramp, a jump over a narrow part of Lime Creek."

"So?"

He cleared his throat again. "So, it ain't just a jump. It's a trap. They got it set up so you can't make that big a jump with all your gear on. You know, the catcher's mask and the shoulder pads and all that cardboard. They figure you won't be able to get up enough speed to clear the jump. You land in the creek, and they got all kinds of stuff buried down there to rip you up—nails, broken glass, pieces of tin, all sorts of junk."

He paused. I didn't say anything.

"Anyway," he went on, "don't let on that you know anything about it. Just play along. And don't let Neal know that Doug said anything."

I nodded. "I won't."

Mama called us to supper. But just as we sat down, the phone rang again. I answered it. It was Gary Pitts. He told me the same thing Larry had and made me swear not to say anything about Doug telling him.

Then Curt Johnson called with the same news, and then Jimmy Jones. I'd barely touched my hamburger steak when it rang again. This time Mama and Dad followed me to the phone. They stood waiting with hands on their hips and irritated looks on their faces while I answered.

"Hello?"

"Pat?" Denny Perrin whispered.

"Yeah?"

"First off, I wanted to tell you I was sorry for

trying to hurt you with the track cleats. It was Neal's idea. I was dumb for letting him talk me into it. You're not still mad at me, are you?"

"No, Denny. I'm not mad. I've let Neal talk me into doing some dumb stuff before too."

"The other reason I called . . ."

He was whispering so softly, I had to shove the phone against my ear so I could hear.

". . . I just found out that Neal and B.B. got this trap set up for you tomorrow. You got to swear that you won't let on that I called. But tomorrow . . ."

Dad cleared his throat. An angry finger jabbed toward the phone. Then his thumb motioned to the dining table.

"I already know about the trap," I told Denny. "Dad wants me to eat my dinner, and I *swear* I won't tell anybody you called. Good-bye."

Dad took the phone off the hook the second I hung up. "That's enough of this phone stuff while we're trying to eat. What's going on?"

I shrugged and tried to look innocent. He glared at me, then all three of us marched back to the dining room. Just as we came through the door, we saw our cat, Mootz. He was perched on the table by Dad's plate, munching Dad's hamburger steak.

Dad's blue eyes turned black as coal.

"Blankety-blank *cat!*" he roared.

He grabbed Mootz by the scruff of his furry neck, marched him to the back door, threw it open (like he had the day I got five stitches in my head), and flung Mootz out into the backyard. Then, still muttering about the blankety-blank cat, he stormed back to the table.

Mama and I didn't say a word. Dad sat down and cut off the edge of his hamburger where Mootz had chewed. Then those black eyes turned toward me.

"Now, about all the phone calls?"

I didn't even think about trying the innocent act. Not after the cat got in his plate. I told Mama and Dad *everything*—from getting stuck under Tiffany Williams's fence to being nicknamed Fat Pat Berry, the Twinkletoes Fairy, then getting my name changed to The Klutz. I told them about the rules to the bet and about the loser having to kiss The Blimp and about the track cleats and about Doug Loy and the football helmet.

By the time I got through, we'd finished supper. Dad seemed a lot calmer, now that he'd eaten. Mama wasn't!

"I'm going to go call Beth Moffett right now," she announced. "I'm going to tell her about this bet and what her son's been doing. We're putting an end to it!"

She sprang up from the table.

"Mama, please don't," I begged.

Dad reached out and caught her by the arm. "Sit down, Toni." He smiled calmly. "Sounds like Pat and his friends are handling the situation."

Mama shook her head. "Why are boys like that? It's bad enough to bet, but doing things that could get Pat hurt . . . Why can't we put an end to this before something serious happens? Why do boys always have to handle things themselves? I really think I should call Mrs. Moffett."

Dad smiled at me. His eyes were blue again. They almost seemed to sparkle. He looked back at Mama and shrugged.

"Boys are boys, Toni," he said. "If Pat wants to handle things himself . . . well, it seems like he's doing fine so far. I think we should let him take care of Neal his own way."

Mama folded her arms and rocked back in her chair.

"It's not fair to Kristine, either," she huffed. "I mean, she's the sweetest girl. . . . It's not right to call her Blimp and make kissing her the penalty for losing some dumb bet."

Dad cocked his eyebrow. "She is a little doll," he agreed.

I jerked when Dad said that. Maybe there was something he could see in Kristine Plimpton—

something under all that fat—that I just couldn't
see. I mean, why else would he call her a little doll?

He turned to me. "Does Kristine know about the
bet?"

"Yes, sir." I nodded.

Dad shrugged again.

"Kristine knows about the bet. Pat's doing fine,
and from all the phone calls he got, it sounds like he
has a lot of friends who are trying to help him. Let's
let him and the boys take care of it."

Mama was still ticked off. Dad patted her on the
arm, trying to calm her. With a jerk of his head he
motioned me to the back door.

"Your mom and I need to talk," he said. "Why
don't you go feed the dog?"

I got up and headed for the door.

"And don't let that *dumb cat* in, either," he
called. Behind me I could still hear him. "Next week
we're leaving for vacation. We'll just take a couple
of extra days. That way we'll get back the Sunday
before Labor Day. Pat won't even be around Neal
Moffett. There's nothing to worry about."

"It's still not right for them to treat Kristine like
that," I heard Mama say as I got the dog food. "Calling her The Blimp. It's just not right."

Chomps's tail thumped against his doghouse

when I set his bowl in front of him. I reached down
and patted his head while he ate.

"I'm gonna beat Neal Moffett," I told Chomps.
Then I looked up at the night sky. It was so clear
and bright, I could see almost every single star.

"Kristine is kinda nice," I confided in him. "And
she's got those brown eyes. . . ."

CHAPTER

17

The following morning at eleven thirty, Neal and Bobby showed up for the game at Doug's house. They had their bicycles and were full of smiles and really excited when they slid to a stop in the driveway.

"Hey, you guys, grab your bikes and come on," Neal called. "B.B. and I made this ramp. We can jump our bikes clear over Lime Creek from the thing. It's ten times more radical than the stuff we had in my backyard."

We all stopped and looked at Neal and B.B. for a moment. Pepper yawned. Kent shrugged his shoulders. Charlie started dribbling the basketball again.

Neal's head cocked to one side. Little lines wrinkled up across his forehead. "Come on, guys. It's totally cool. I ain't kiddin'."

Doug was standing by the basketball goal, trying not to be noticed. José was next to him. Doug didn't say a word, but José waved his arms and pointed at Neal.

"Fine, Doug!" he almost roared. "You want to go with them, go right ahead. The rest of us are gonna play basketball."

Doug looked a little startled. Then, realizing what José was up to, he almost smiled. "Well, it really sounds like fun," he lied. "But if none of the rest of you want to go . . . well . . ."

"Let's keep playing." Larry laughed as he stole the ball from Charlie and shot a basket. "Tiffany will probably be out to suntan. She's a lot more interesting than trying to jump over Lime Creek on a bicycle."

Everyone laughed and went back to the game.

Bobby got nervous. He started wiping his nose on his sleeve. The smile left Neal's face, and he turned beet red from his forehead clear down to the tips of his fingers.

"You all are on Pat's side, aren't you? You're always siding with him. You all are nothing but a bunch of cowards. You're a bunch of fairies, just like The Klutz."

His eyes scrunched to tiny slits. The red left his face, and he turned pale. Neal Moffett looked straight at me. He shook so hard it looked like an earthquake was going on inside him.

"Besides, I don't care if I lose the dumb bet," he roared. "Pat could never kiss The Blimp anyway. He's chicken."

Neal puffed air into his cheeks, blowing them up like balloons. He arched his back so his stomach stuck out, making him look fat. "If The Klutz tried to kiss The Blimp, he'd probably pass out or something." Then he yanked his bike from the ground. "I can do it though. I ain't scared to kiss The Blimp. You guys are a bunch of jerks, but everybody else at Hoover's gonna get a big kick out of it. I'll have 'em laughing their heads off. I might even act like I'm gonna throw up after I kiss her. It's gonna be hilarious."

With that he jumped on his bike and took off. Bobby was the only one who followed him.

Nobody saw Neal or Bobby for a whole week. Some of the guys rode by Neal's house on the way to Doug's for basketball, but they never saw him playing in his yard.

I figured my life would be easier with Neal out of sight.

Wrong.

Before, only Kent and José had gone with me everywhere I went. Now I was surrounded by *all* the guys. They wanted to be sure I didn't have an accident.

José's parents took him to Colorado for a week. But when Kent arrived to take me to the high-school weight room, eight or nine guys came with him. When we went to McDonald's, all the guys who had an allowance or whose folks had given them some money went, too. I couldn't even walk home without a bunch of guys escorting me to the front door. One day Charlie and Pepper jumped in front of me and almost knocked me down because they thought I hadn't seen the little red wagon the Bertwilder twins had left on the sidewalk. They didn't want to take a chance that I might trip over it.

It was ridiculous!

I was starting to feel like the president of the United States. I mean, if the guys had worn suits and carried walkie-talkies, they would have looked like Secret Service men or CIA agents. It was sickening. I couldn't even peek over the fence at Tiffany Williams without having four or five people standing beside me. It almost drove Butch and Ben crazy.

When that week was up and it was time to leave for Galveston, Texas, for vacation, I was the happiest kid in the world. I was sick of having that many people around me all the time. I could hardly wait for a few days—*alone!*

José got home from his vacation before I left. He warned me to be careful when I crossed the street and to be extremely careful about stepping on broken glass at the beach.

"What if I drown in the ocean?" I asked.

José just laughed. "That's okay. Just so long as you don't break anything or get stitches."

Nothing like having such a good friend!

I loved the beach. The water at Galveston isn't all that clear or pretty, but I had fun. We ate at neat places, we swam, and we hunted for seashells. We stayed at this really cool motel. It was built on cement stilts and stuck way out into the water. Mama and I bought three loaves of bread from a corner store. We stood on the little balcony outside our room and tossed the bread in the air. The sea gulls swooped down and caught it before it hit the water. We held it out instead of throwing it, and some swooped down and took it right out of our hands. We had a ball. We got home Sunday night, before Labor Day.

*   *   *

On Labor Day, I went to José's. It was a little too early for us to go to Doug's yard and see if Tiffany Williams had grown any during the week I was gone, so we read some of José's comics.

He didn't ask if I'd had a good time. He didn't even notice the great tan I had gotten. He just sort of looked me over real good to see if I had any stitches or anything broken.

Like I said, it's great to have such good friends.

About twelve, we went to Kent's. Then the three of us headed for Doug Loy's house. Kent wanted to know if I'd met any cute girls while I was in Galveston. José didn't care if I'd met any. He just wanted to hear about the bikinis and what the girls looked like.

"You're gonna do it, Pat," Kent said, patting me on the back. "You're gonna beat ol' Neal. He's gonna have to kiss The Blimp."

"Her name's Kristine," I muttered.

Neither one of them heard me. We rounded the corner by the Bertwilders' house. One of the twins had left a roller skate on the sidewalk. I saw it as soon as we turned the corner.

I guess José didn't think I'd noticed it, because when we got close, he jumped in front of me.

"Careful," José said. "Don't trip over—"

Just as he stepped in front of me, I heard this sound. It was kind of a *twing* or *ping* sound. It was a funny little noise, like a spring popping or snapping. A little *poof* sound followed it.

José never finished what he was saying. The instant I saw him cut in front of me, the instant I heard that strange sound, José screamed. He grabbed his right eye and fell to his knees on the sidewalk.

CHAPTER

18

"It was a BB gun," Kent's voice roared. "He shot José's eye out with a BB gun. I'll kill him!"

I dropped to my knees beside José. I could hear the sound of shoes racing down the sidewalk. I didn't look up. Instead I tried to move my friend's hands so I could see.

José kept pushing me back. Finally I got his hands away from his eye. But when I reached toward him, he pushed my hands aside once more.

"I can get it," I said, trying to make him let go. Gentle as I could, I touched his cheek.

"Be real still," I urged. "It's right below your eye. I can get it."

Carefully I squeezed the little knot at the bridge of his cheekbone. A tiny bronze ball slipped out.

The BB rolled around in the palm of my hand. I held it out for José to see.

"It's okay, José. It hit your cheek. Can you see all right?"

José rubbed at the little knot below his eye. He blinked a couple of times, then smiled.

"Yeah. It stings, but I can see just fine."

I shook my head. The chills made my shoulders squeeze together.

"Man, that was close. Another inch and it would have . . ."

The words, the thought, stuck in my throat like peanut butter sticks to the roof of my mouth. Another inch and José would have lost his eye. All he was trying to do was keep me from tripping over a roller skate, and he almost got his eye shot out.

A puff of red smoke clouded my vision.

"It was meant for me," I whispered. "José almost got blinded on account of me and this dumb bet."

Somehow I was on my feet. I started walking. I didn't run. I walked.

Behind me I could hear José's footsteps. I kept walking.

When José and I rounded the corner, we could see the guys standing in Doug's driveway. We could hear Kent yelling, almost screaming.

"Let me go. I'm gonna kill that . . ."

Skinny as he was, it took five guys to hold Kent Green. He kept slinging his arms, trying to wiggle loose from their grasp so he could get at Neal. I'd seen José act like that, but I'd never seen Kent that mad in his whole life.

"I been here all morning!" Neal Moffett shouted above the commotion. "Ask Doug. Ask Charlie—he was here, too."

All Kent said was, "I'm gonna kill him."

Doug and Charlie both nodded. "He really was," they confessed. "He's been here since nine. It wasn't him."

I didn't break my stride. I just kept walking.

"Where's B.B.?" José snarled from behind me. "Where's your snot-nosed little friend, Neal?"

Everybody sort of looked around.

José went flying past me, into the group. "You coward!" José screamed. "You're always calling everybody else chicken, but you're too much of a coward to do your own dirty work. You sent Bobby and his BB gun after Pat. He missed and hit me instead. I'm gonna . . ."

The guys who weren't holding Kent grabbed José as he waded into the gang.

At the edge of the group, I stopped. Everybody

looked at me. Neal Moffett had that big-shot, self-confident sneer on his face. He was the best athlete in Hoover Middle School. He was cool and strong and nobody messed with Neal Moffett.

I was The Klutz—I was Fat Pat Berry, the Twinkletoes Fairy.

My eyes clouded. I felt the tears roll down my cheeks. I tasted the salt in the corners of my mouth.

"You hurt my friend."

That's all I said. Then . . .

I started toward him. One step at a time.

I didn't care that Neal Moffett was probably going to beat me to a pulp in front of all my friends. I didn't care that Tiffany Williams was watching from her air mattress and would probably tell all her friends about it, too. All I thought about was how Neal hurt José.

Neal drew his fists up.

"I'll rip your head off, Berry. I'll beat the tar out of you."

I kept walking.

I guess there was something else in my eyes besides tears. A look—something—because just when I was almost to him, Neal Moffett—the coolest, strongest, best athlete at Hoover Middle School—broke and ran.

He just spun around on his toes and took off. He raced across Doug Loy's backyard and leaped Tiffany Williams's fence.

I went after him.

I hopped over the fence by Doug's pecan tree. Neal climbed the fence at the far side of Tiffany's yard. Butch and Ben were hot on his heels. His pants leg caught on the top of the fence. He fell, but scrambled quickly to his feet and raced up the alley. Butch and Ben charged for me. I ignored them. Then Butch latched onto my leg. I kicked sideways. There was kind of a squeal, then a splash. Behind me I could hear the other guys climbing the fence.

Neal stumbled and sprinted down the alley. I jumped the fence at the far side of Tiffany's yard. At the end of the alley, Neal dodged around his basketball net and raced for his back door, hard as he could run. Puffing and out of breath, he slowed down about halfway across his yard.

The time I'd spent with Kent and José running around the track was paying off. Not even breathing hard, I closed the distance between Neal and me.

His eyes flashed wide when he saw me coming. He raced to his house. He jumped the three steps at the back door and slipped inside. He latched the screen just as I reached the door.

I yanked on the handle. It didn't budge. I bit down on my lip and yanked harder. The handle almost came off in my hand.

"Open it!" I snarled like some half-crazed mad dog.

Frantically Neal shook his head. "No way!" he huffed. "You got the whole gang after me. I can't fight all of you."

I glanced over my shoulder. Most of the guys had caught up with us. They stood watching in the middle of the yard.

"This is between me and Neal," I said. "You guys stay out of it."

They nodded, and I turned back to the screen.

"Just you and me, Neal. Open the door!"

Neal made a gulping sound when he swallowed. Then he tried to look tough. "What if I bust your lip, Klutz? What if you have to get stitches?" He puffed his cheeks out and arched his back so he'd look fat. "The Klutz kissing The Blimp. Don't that scare you, Berry?"

I let go of the handle. My fists drew up at my sides.

"Open the door!"

"You might not be scared of me," Neal scoffed. "But think about kissing The Blimp. She's a perfect match for you, Berry. You're both nothin' but a couple of big fat hogs." He made a snorting sound with his nose. "You two are a couple of regular porkers. You make the perfect pair."

Something snapped.

I didn't think about it, it just happened.

Suddenly my fist was no longer clenched at my side. It was going through the screen. The wire ripped, and the instant my hand broke through, I grabbed Neal's T-shirt. If he wasn't going to come out and face me, I was planning to drag him out.

A gasp came from the gang of guys behind me. Neal's eyes jumped out of their sockets. I hung onto the shirt. A little squeak rose in his throat. He jerked and spun around. The shirt ripped, and he raced away from the door.

"Mommy! Mommy, *help!*"

His voice faded as he disappeared into another room.

I pulled my arm and Neal's shirt back through the screen. Another gasp came from the gang of guys. Then I heard someone moan, "Oh, no!"

"Oh, Pat . . ." another whispered.

I turned to see what their problem was. All the guys stood watching me. Their mouths were wide open. Their eyes were welded to me in stark horror.

I frowned.

José, still holding one hand over the knot under

his eye, pointed. "Your arm, Pat." He breathed. "Your arm."

I looked down. I rolled my arm to the side so my palm was up. Little drops of red trickled down. A cut, halfway between my wrist and elbow and about three inches long, leaked blood. Red drops rolled down my arm and dripped off my fingers.

CHAPTER

19

It was a sad, somber group that walked the three blocks to my house. No one talked. Well, almost no one. At the corner where the Bertwilder twins lived, José nudged me with his elbow. He pointed back at Curt Johnson. Curt looked a little pale. He shuffled along with eyes wide and his hands hanging limp by his sides.

"Can't believe it," he gasped. "Can't believe I yelled, and you guys didn't even turn around and look."

He sighed. His eyes rolled in his head.

"I mean—there she was—when we all went crashing over that fence, she just sat straight up. Didn't get her pink top off the mattress or anything. She just sat up." His eyes got wide again. He raised his limp hands. "I mean . . . all of her . . . right there in front of my eyes . . . and you guys didn't even look back. . . . I can't believe it. . . ."

Curt Johnson was so pale, I thought the guys were going to have to help him home instead of me.

Mama didn't panic when they brought me to the house. She just looked at my arm and called Dad. He drove me to the emergency room at the hospital.

Dad had to fill out some papers. Then a nurse took us to one of the little rooms. She stuck a thermometer in my mouth and had me step onto the scales. As if I didn't feel bad enough already, it was really great to see that I weighed exactly the same as I had when summer started. It made me so mad, I could hardly see straight.

"What's with you, Pat?"

Dad's voice startled me. "Huh?"

"What are you upset about?" he asked. "Your bottom lip looks like it's fixing to scrape the floor."

I pulled the thermometer out of my mouth. "My weight."

"What about your weight?"

"I've been eating right all summer. I've been running and lifting weights, but every time I get on the scales—nothing. I weigh just the same as I did when summer started."

Dad giggled.

"It's not funny," I pouted. "No matter what I do, I guess I'll always be fat."

"I wasn't laughing at you, Pat." He folded his arms. "You're not fat anymore. You're a good four to six inches taller now than you were at the first of summer, and you're solid as a rock. You may weigh the same, but it's not fat. How long's it been since you looked in a mirror? You're growing up, son."

I didn't answer him. I hadn't spent much time looking in a mirror since third grade. I guess that's because I never liked what I saw. Sure, I always combed my hair before school, but I got dressed first. That's because every time I looked in a mirror, Fat Pat Berry, the Twinkletoes Fairy was staring back.

"You really don't think I'm fat?"

Dad smiled. "Muscle weighs more than fat. Besides, like I said, you're a whole lot taller and . . ."

The nurse came in and we stopped talking. She got this orange stuff and scrubbed my arm. It stung a little but it wasn't bad. When she had most of the dried blood washed away, the gash didn't look nearly as deep as I had thought. It was still bad, though.

She left and the doctor came in. Dad stood in a corner of the room while the doctor twisted my arm one way, then the other. He squeezed the edge of the cut together. He frowned, then scratched his head.

"Well, not too bad," he said. "Don't really know what would work best, Mr. Berry."

I thought he was talking to Dad until he looked me straight in the eye.

"Figure a couple of butterfly bandages or some strip tape might work. Then again, to be on the safe side, two or three stitches would hold better. What do you think, Mr. Berry?"

Again he wasn't talking to Dad. He was looking me square in the eye. I didn't know what to say.

I closed my eyes.

And in that instant I could see The Blimp's fat lips coming at me. I could see the whole school laughing.

I looked at my arm, then closed my eyes again.

And I could see Neal Moffett. I could see his cheeks puffed out to make his face look fat. I could see him arch his back so his tummy looked big and round. I could hear him making that snorting sound with his nose, grunting like a pig. I could see everybody laughing at Kristine and those big brown eyes of hers filling up with tears and . . .

I forced my eyes open. I swallowed the big knot in my throat and looked at the doctor.

"Stitches."

CHAPTER

20

Dad never said a word as he drove me home. But for the first time in my life, I felt like he was proud of me.

Why—I didn't know.

I'd lost the bet with Neal. I had four stitches in my arm. I was going to have to kiss The Blimp. Kiss her in front of the whole school. But inside I felt good.

Why—I didn't know that, either.

There was one thing I *did* know. I could never tell anyone that the doctor gave me a choice and I said, "Stitches." I couldn't explain it to myself, much less to the guys. José was my best friend. He was the only one who knew the *real* reason I fainted when the nurse X-rayed my ribs. I'd told him about seeing Kristine's pudgy cheeks and fat lips coming at me, and how I'd panicked. José hadn't told anyone.

But I couldn't even tell José about having a choice between strip tape and stitches. It made me feel a little lonely.

The guys were hanging all over our front porch when we drove up. They charged Dad's truck like a cavalry troop. When I held my arms out and showed them the stitches, they slumped. Then, one at a time, they left. Even Kent and José, my best friends, walked away.

Now I really felt lonely.

Mama met us at the front door. She looked worried. Then I found out she wasn't worried about my stitches.

"Neal Moffett's mother called," she told Dad. "She's very upset about the broken screen and her son's torn shirt. I think you should call her, Paul."

Dad shook his head.

"Not right now. If I call her now, I'll tell her where she can stick that shirt and the screen both!"

He glanced over at me. Then his chest puffed out big as a barrel. "We got us a pretty good young man here, Toni," he told Mama. "Think I'll charcoal him a big, lean steak for supper. He's worth it." He slugged me on the shoulder. "And if Beth Moffett want us to buy her a new screen . . . well, he's worth that, too."

Mama started asking Dad what happened. He told her to come out and help him get the charcoal going and he'd tell her. I went up to my room to change my clothes.

Mama and Dad were extra nice to me at supper. Dad even fed Chomps for me. Mama told me that Kristine Plimpton had just gotten home from camp and had called while we were at the emergency room. When Mama told her about my arm, Kristine said she hoped I wasn't hurt bad, but she sure wished I'd lost the bet.

Mama and Dad being nice to me made me feel good. Finding out that Kristine had called made my stomach tie up in a knot. I hardly ate any of my steak.

Being deserted by all my friends on account of losing a dumb bet made me feel even worse.

I almost fell down the steps the next morning when I opened the front door and found the whole gang waiting in my yard. They walked me to school.

Rick Davis even moved the Bertwilder twins' roller skates off the sidewalk when we got to their corner.

"After you headed to the doctor's," they told me, "we went after Bobby Blaton. The Blatons moved. The house was empty, and there's a for-sale sign in the front yard."

Charlie Ratcliff found some BBs in the trash behind their house. Gary Pitts said he'd seen Bobby's parents following the moving van and that B.B. was playing with a stopwatch. It had a black strap just like the one Neal's dad had given Neal.

"If we could just catch B.B.," Pepper Young said, "I'd make him confess. I'd sit on his stomach until he—"

"No!" I cut him off. "Neal didn't stick my arm through the screen. He didn't make me get stitches. I lost. It's over."

Heads bowed, they followed me to school.

I guess most everybody in school already knew about the bet. The ones who didn't know, Neal had probably told before we got there. Usually there were little clumps of students all over the place. Some hung out on the sides of the building, some by the teachers' parking lot, others waited for the doors to open on the basketball court. This morning *everybody* at Hoover Middle School was standing near the front door.

Neal Moffett was right in the center of things. Even before we got there, I could hear him laughing. He made that noise that sounded like a pig grunting.

A sudden silence fell when we walked up the steps. The smile on Neal's face stretched from ear to ear.

"Hear you got stitches yesterday, Berry. You were the biggest klutz in fifth grade. Nice to know you're gonna be the same guy in sixth."

José lunged toward him.

"You'd be the one with stitches," he shouted loud enough for everyone to hear. "If you hadn't run home to your *mommy*, Pat woulda . . ."

I caught my friend's arm. Neal rocked back and laughed. "I can hardly wait for The Blimp to come floating in," he said, quickly changing the subject. He puffed his cheeks out and arched his back. Then he started whispering stuff to the group of people gathered around him. He laughed, and every now and then I heard him *oink-oink*.

Neal and most of the kids stood on the left side of the front doors. José, Kent, and all the rest of the guys stood with me on the right.

Waiting was the hardest part.

It was almost time for the bell when José pulled me aside. "Are you sure you can do it, Pat?"

I shrugged.

José's eyebrow dipped. "I mean . . ." He looked around to make sure no one else was listening. "Remember the X-ray room? What if you faint?"

"I won't. Kristine's got great eyes. I figure all I got to do is forget about the rest of her. It doesn't matter how fat she is. I just have to concentrate on those brown eyes and . . ."

A sudden silence fell across the school grounds like a giant wave crashing on the beach. I looked past José. The Plimptons' station wagon pulled to a stop in the circle drive.

"Brown eyes," I told myself. "Nothing but brown eyes."

The bell rang and Freddie Kruger unlocked the front doors. Nobody moved. The door of the station wagon opened.

"Brown eyes," I repeated inside my head as I waited for Kristine's short little pudgy legs to appear.

The car door swung wide. Only short little pudgy legs didn't appear. Instead two long, slender, luscious legs kind of unfolded from the front seat. A girl got out. She had on a black dress. It was one of those knit things that clung.

This one clung—to all the right places.

"Golleeeee!" Curt Johnson breathed from someplace behind me. "That can't be . . . golly!"

The tall, slender girl with a black dress and a *fantastic* figure closed the Plimptons' car door and strolled gracefully toward the school.

Sweat popped out on José's brow.

"I think Kristine changed some . . . I think," José said.

I shook my head. Then those brown eyes caught mine. Those eyes that twinkle. Those brown eyes that could laugh at me and cut right into me.

Sure enough, those eyes belonged to the tall, slender girl with the legs and all the *great* curves.

Kristine walked right up to me. Those eyes kind of looked me up and down. They seemed to twinkle even more.

"You changed some this summer." She traced her tongue across those full, pouting lips. "You've lost weight or gotten taller or something. Nice!"

I couldn't say anything.

Kristine took a deep breath. I almost fainted.

"Hear you lost the bet." She sighed.

I just stood there looking at her. I'd gotten myself

all worked up—all ready and prepared to kiss The Blimp. This wasn't The Blimp. This girl was the most beautiful, gorgeous, curvy creature anyone at Hoover Middle School had ever seen.

Kristine Plimpton winked. Then she held her arms out.

"Well? . . ."

I guess I would have stood there all day with my mouth gaping open if it hadn't been for my best friend.

José gouged me in the back with his thumb. "The eyes, Pat," he whispered. "Remember? Just the eyes."

I raised my hands, not knowing what to do with them. I just sort of stood there like a robot. Kristine put my left hand around her back and my right hand on her shoulder. Then she moved closer. I felt weak and shaky.

"The eyes," José whispered.

I liked Kristine's eyes. Holding a girl in my arms wasn't as bad as I thought. In fact, it felt kind of good.

There must have been four hundred people on the steps of Hoover Middle School. If a butterfly had landed on the sidewalk, everyone would have heard it—that's how quiet it was. Freddie Kruger didn't even rattle the door and yell for us to come inside.

Kristine stretched up on her tiptoes. Her soft, full lips moved gently toward mine. I forced myself to think about *nothing* but her eyes.

Then our lips touched.

It was the first time I ever kissed a girl. I felt funny all over. It was a good kind of funny though. Kissing wasn't nearly as bad as I thought it would be.

Like Kristine, I had my eyes closed. I heard some of the girls coo. Some of the guys yelled out:

"Way to go, Pat."

"All right, Berry!"

Everybody clapped and cheered. Then, above the commotion, we could hear Freddie Kruger shout:

"Enough of this stuff. Everybody into the building."

The whole school waited for us to walk inside first. Then everyone followed us down the hall. Everyone, that is, except Neal Moffett. When we went inside the school, Neal was kind of propped up in the corner by the front door. He was white as a ghost. It looked like any second his leg might give way and he'd sink down in the corner like a discarded piece of crumpled notebook paper.

Kristine held my hand as we walked toward our lockers. It felt good to hold her hand. She kept talking about how much I'd changed over the summer. I kept trying not to watch the way that black knit dress clung to her curves.

"I'm glad you lost the bet," she whispered.

I wanted to say "Me too," but all I could muster was a weak little smile.

"Mr. Paramore's starting dance class next week," she said. "Tiffany's thinking about joining. You're still going to come, aren't you?"

Again, all I could do was smile and nod.

Kristine got her notebook and headed for her first-hour class. As she moved down the hall, I couldn't help watching the black dress and the curves. All of a sudden my head felt light. I could feel myself rock back and forth.

Herb Scott's locker was next to mine. I don't know whether he saw me wobbling or not, but suddenly he grabbed hold of me. I caught my balance and forced my eyes from the tight black dress.

"How does a guy go about getting into your dance class?" Herb asked.

Before school was out that day, seven more guys asked me the same question.

With school starting and homework and stuff, there wasn't much chance to play. The guys did manage to get together on Saturday. We met at twelve noon in Doug Loy's driveway to play basketball.

Neal wasn't there. Nobody really cared, though. Neal was no longer interesting.

What *was* interesting were the three girls suntanning in Tiffany's pool.

Terri Laughton rolled over on her stomach and unsnapped her top. Nobody got excited. She was still straight and skinny, like last year.

Tiffany Williams rolled over and did the same thing. We all held our breath.

But when Kristine Plimpton reached back for the strap on her white bikini, the basketball game *stopped*!

All the guys walked to the fence like a bunch of zombies. We hung over the top rail and gaped.

The rail was bent from where the guys had followed me the day I jumped over it to chase Neal Moffett home. Butch and Ben saw us coming. They started to bark, but when Ben saw me, he tucked in his little fluff tail and went running to his doghouse. Butch followed.

We stood there kind of drooling over the chain-link fence for a while. José leaned toward my ear.

"I can't believe how much Kristine Plimpton grew up this summer," he whispered. "Next to her, even Tiffany Williams isn't much anymore. I bet she kisses great, too. Doesn't she?"

I didn't answer.

"I mean, it looked like a nice kiss—a *great* kiss. What was it like?"

There are some things you can't explain, not even to your best friend.

"Let's go finish the game" was all I said. I turned and left the fence. But when I looked around for the ball, I couldn't find it.

Just about then I heard a splash.

"Whoops," Jimmy Jones called. "I dropped the basketball. I'll go and get it."

"Never mind," I heard Tiffany call back. "I'll get it for you."

I glanced over my shoulder. Never rising so much as a fraction of an inch off the mattress, Tiffany got the ball with one hand and threw it. A perfect hook shot, it flew right into Jimmy's arms.

Then I heard Curt Johnson's mournful cry:

"How do girls do that?"

ABOUT THE AUTHOR

BILL WALLACE lives outside Chickasha, Oklahoma, on a farm, where he has five dogs, three cats, and two horses. When not answering letters from children, spending time with his wife, children, and grandchildren, he works on his books. *Beauty* (winner of the Kansas William Allen White Award, and the Oklahoma Sequoyah Award); *The Biggest Klutz in the Fifth Grade; Buffalo Gal, The Christmas Spurs; Danger in Quicksand Swamp* (winner of the Pacific Northwest Young Readers' Choice Award); *Danger on Panther Peak* (original title: *Shadow on the Snow*); *A Dog Called Kitty* (winner of the Nebraska Golden Sower Award, the Oklahoma Sequoyah Award, and the Texas Bluebonnet Award); *Ferret in the Bedroom, Lizards in the Fridge* (winner of the Nebraska Golden Sower Award and the South Carolina Children's Book Award); *Snot Stew* (winner of the South Carolina Children's Book Award, and the Texas Bluebonnet Award); and *Totally Disgusting!* are available from Minstrel Books. *Trapped in Death Cave* (winner of the Florida Sunshine State Young Readers' Award, the Utah Children's Book Award, and the Wyoming Soaring Eagle Book Award) and *Red Dog* are available from Archway Paperbacks.